Also by Jean Rhys and
available in Popular Library editions:

TIGERS ARE BETTER-LOOKING
VOYAGE IN THE DARK
WIDE SARGASSO SEA

JEAN RHYS

SLEEP IT OFF, LADY

POPULAR LIBRARY • NEW YORK

Published by Popular Library, a unit of CBS Publications,
the Consumer Publishing Division of CBS Inc.,
by arrangement with Harper & Row Publishers, Inc.

April, 1978

Library of Congress Catalog Card Number: 74-15889

ISBN: 0-445-04208-7

"Pioneers, Oh, Pioneers" was first published in *The Times* (London)
under the title "Dear Darling Mr. Ramage".

"Sleep It Off, Lady" was first published in *The New Review.*

"The Insect World" was first published in England in
The Sunday Times Magazine and first published in the United States
in *Mademoiselle.*

"Goodbye Marcus, Goodbye Rose", "Heat", "Kikimora", and
"On Not Shooting Sitting Birds" were first published in
The New Yorker.

Contents

Pioneers, Oh, Pioneers

As the two girls were walking up yellow-hot Market Street, Irene nudged her sister and said: "Look at her!"

They were not far from the market, they could still smell the fish.

When Rosalie turned her head the few white women she saw carried parasols. The black women were barefooted, wore gaily striped turbans and highwaisted dresses. It was still the nineteenth century, November 1899.

"There she goes," said Irene.

And there was Mrs. Menzies, riding up to her house on the Morne for a cool weekend.

"Good morning," Rosalie said, but Mrs. Menzies did not answer. She rode past, clip-clop, clip-clop, in her thick, dark riding habit brought from England ten years before, balancing a large dripping parcel wrapped in flannel on her knee.

"It's ice. She wants her drinks cold," said Rosalie.

"Why can't she have it sent up like everybody else? The black people laugh at her. She ought to be ashamed of herself."

"I don't see why," Rosalie said obstinately.

"Oh, you," Irene jeered. "You like crazy people. You like Jimmy Longa and you like old maman Menzies. You liked Ramage, nasty beastly horrible Ramage."

Rosalie said: "You cried about him yesterday."

"Yesterday doesn't count. Mother says we were all hysterical yesterday."

By this time they were nearly home so Rosalie said nothing. But she put her tongue out as they went up the steps into the long, cool gallery.

Their father, Dr. Cox, was sitting in an armchair with a three-legged table by his side.

On the table were his pipe, his tin of tobacco and his glasses. Also *The Times* weekly edition, the *Cornhill Magazine*, the *Lancet* and a West Indian newspaper, the *Dominica Herald and Leeward Islands Gazette*.

He was not to be spoken to, as they saw at once though one was only eleven and the other nine.

"Dead as a door nail," he muttered as they went past him into the next room so comfortably full of rocking chairs, a mahogany

table, palm leaf fans, a tigerskin rug, family
photographs, views of Bettws-y-Coed and a
large picture of wounded soldiers in the snow,
Napoleon's Retreat from Moscow.

The doctor had not noticed his daughters, for
he too was thinking about Mr. Ramage. He
had liked the man, stuck up for him, laughed
off his obvious eccentricities, denied point
blank that he was certifiable. All wrong.
Ramage, probably a lunatic, was now as dead
as a door nail. Nothing to be done.

Ramage had first arrived in the island two
years before, a handsome man in tropical kit,
white suit, red cummerbund, solar topee.
After he grew tired of being followed about
by an admiring crowd of little Negro boys he
stopped wearing the red sash and the solar
topee but he clung to his white suits though
most of the men wore dark trousers even
when the temperature was ninety in the
shade.

Miss Lambton, who had been a fellow pas-
senger from Barbados, reported that he was
certainly a gentleman and also a king among
men when it came to looks. But he was very
unsociable. He ignored all invitations to
dances, tennis parties and moonlight picnics.
He never went to church and was not to be
seen at the club. He seemed to like Dr. Cox,
however, and dined with him one evening.
And Rosalie, then aged seven, fell in love.

After dinner, though the children were not supposed to talk much when guests were there, and were usually not allowed downstairs at all, she edged up to him and said: "Sing something." (People who came to dinner often sang afterwards, as she well knew.)

"I can't sing," said Ramage.

"Yes you can." Her mother's disapproving expression made her insist the more. "You can. You can."

He laughed and hoisted her on to his knee. With her head against his chest she listened while he rumbled gently: "Baa baa black sheep, have you any wool? Yes sir, yes sir, three bags full."

Then the gun at the fort fired for nine o'clock and the girls, smug in their stiff white dresses, had to say goodnight nicely and go upstairs to bed.

After a perfunctory rubber of whist with a dummy, Mrs. Cox also departed. Over his whisky and soda Ramage explained that he'd come to the island with the intention of buying an estate. "Small, and as remote as possible."

"That won't be difficult here."

"So I heard," said Ramage.

"Tried any of the other islands?"

"I went to Barbados first."

"Little England," the doctor said. "Well?"

"I was told that there were several places

going along this new Imperial Road you've
got here."

"Won't last," Dr. Cox said. "Nothing lasts in
this island. Nothing will come of it. You'll
see."

Ramage looked puzzled.

"It's all a matter of what you want the
place for," the doctor said without explaining
himself. "Are you after a good interest on
your capital or what?"

"Peace," Ramage said. "Peace, that's what
I'm after."

"You'll have to pay for that," the doctor
said.

"What's the price?" said Ramage, smiling.
He put one leg over the other. His bare ankle
was hairy and thin, his hands long and slender
for such a big man.

"You'll be very much alone."

"That will suit me," Ramage said.

"And if you're far along the road, you'll
have to cut the trees down, burn the stumps
and start from scratch."

"Isn't there a half-way house?" Ramage
said.

The doctor answered rather vaguely: "You
might be able to get hold of one of the older
places."

He was thinking of young Errington, of
young Kellaway, who had both bought estates
along the Imperial Road and worked hard.
But they had given up after a year or two,

sold their land cheap and gone back to England. They could not stand the loneliness and melancholy of the forest.

A fortnight afterwards Miss Lambton told Mrs. Cox that Mr. Ramage had bought Spanish Castle, the last but one of the older properties. It was beautiful but not prosperous —some said bad luck, others bad management. His nearest neighbour was Mr. Eliot, who owned *Malgré Tout*. Now called Twickenham.

For several months after this Ramage disappeared and one afternoon at croquet Mrs. Cox asked Miss Lambton if she had any news of him.

"A strange man," she said, "very reserved."

"Not so reserved as all that," said Miss Lambton. "He got married several weeks ago. He told me that he didn't want it talked about."

"No!" said Mrs. Cox. "Who to?"

Then it all came out. Ramage had married a coloured girl who called herself Isla Harrison, though she had no right to the name of Harrison. Her mother was dead and she'd been brought up by her godmother, old Miss Myra, according to local custom. Miss Myra kept a sweet shop in Bay Street and Isla was very well known in the town—too well known.

"He took her to Trinidad," said Miss Lambton mournfully, "and when they came back they were married. They went down to Spanish Castle and I've heard nothing about them since."

"It's not as though she was a nice coloured girl," everybody said.

So the Ramages were lost to white society. Lost to everyone but Dr. Cox. Spanish Castle estate was in a district which he visited every month, and one afternoon as he was driving past he saw Ramage standing near his letter box which was nailed to a tree visible from the road. He waved. Ramage waved back and beckoned.

While they were drinking punch on the verandah, Mrs. Ramage came in. She was dressed up to the nines, smelt very strongly of cheap scent and talked loudly in an aggressive voice. No, she certainly wasn't a nice coloured girl.

The doctor tried—too hard perhaps—for the next time he called at Spanish Castle a door banged loudly inside the house and a grinning boy told him that Mr. Ramage was out.

"And Mrs. Ramage?"

"The mistress is not at home."

At the end of the path the doctor looked back and saw her at a window peering at him.

He shook his head, but he never went there again, and the Ramage couple sank out of sight, out of mind.

It was Mr. Eliot, the owner of Twickenham, who started the trouble. He was out with his wife, he related, looking at some young nutmeg trees near the boundary. They had a boy with them who had lighted a fire and put on water for tea. They looked up and saw Ramage coming out from under the trees. He was burnt a deep brown, his hair fell to his shoulders, his beard to his chest. He was wearing sandals and a leather belt, on one side of which hung a cutlass, on the other a large pouch. Nothing else.

"If," said Mr. Eliot, "the man had apologized to my wife, if he'd shown the slightest consciousness of the fact that he was stark naked, I would have overlooked the whole thing. God knows one learns to be tolerant in this wretched place. But not a bit of it. He stared hard at her and came out with: 'What an uncomfortable dress—and how ugly!' My wife got very red. Then she said: 'Mr. Ramage, the kettle is just boiling. Will you have some tea?'"

"Good for her," said the doctor. "What did he say to that?"

"Well, he seemed rather confused. He bowed from the waist, exactly as if he had clothes on, and explained that he never drank tea. 'I have a stupid habit of talking to myself. I beg your pardon,' he said, and off he went. We got home and my wife locked herself in the bedroom. When she came out she wouldn't speak to me at first, then she said that he was quite right, I didn't care what she looked like, so now she didn't either. She called me a mean man. A mean man. I won't have it," said Mr. Eliot indignantly. "He's mad, walking about with a cutlass. He's dangerous."

"Oh, I don't think so," said Dr. Cox. "He'd probably left his clothes round the corner and didn't know how to explain. Perhaps we do cover ourselves up too much. The sun can be good for you. The best thing in the world. If you'd seen as I have. . . ."

Mr. Eliot interrupted at once. He knew that when the doctor started talking about his unorthodox methods he went on for a long time.

"I don't know about all that. But I may as well tell you that I dislike the idea of a naked man with a cutlass wandering about near my place. I dislike it very much indeed. I've got to consider my wife and my daughter. Something ought to be done."

Eliot told his story to everyone who'd listen and the Ramages became the chief topic of conversation.

"It seems," Mrs. Cox told her husband, "that he does wear a pair of trousers as a rule and even an old coat when it rains, but several people have watched him lying in a hammock on the verandah naked. You ought to call there and speak to him. They say," she added, "that the two of them fight like Kilkenny cats. He's making himself very unpopular."

So the next time he visited the district Dr. Cox stopped near Spanish Castle. As he went up the garden path he noticed how unkempt and deserted the place looked. The grass on the lawn had grown very high and the verandah hadn't been swept for days.

The doctor paused uncertainly, then tapped on the sitting-room door, which was open. "Hallo," called Ramage from inside the house, and he appeared, smiling. He was wearing one of his linen suits, clean and pressed, and his hair and beard were trimmed.

"You're looking very well," the doctor said.

"Oh, yes, I feel splendid. Sit down and I'll get you a drink."

There seemed to be no one else in the house.

"The servants have all walked out," Ramage explained when he appeared with the punch.

"Good Lord, have they?"

· "Yes, but I think I've found an old woman in the village who'll come up and cook."

"And how is Mrs. Ramage?"

At this moment there was a heavy thud on the side of the house, then another, then another.

"What was that?" asked Dr. Cox.

"Somebody throwing stones. They do sometimes."

"Why, in heaven's name?"

"I don't know. Ask them."

Then the doctor repeated Eliot's story, but in spite of himself it came out as trivial, even jocular.

"Yes, I was very sorry about that," Ramage answered casually. "They startled me as much as I startled them. I wasn't expecting to see anyone. It was a bit of bad luck but it won't happen again."

"It was bad luck meeting Eliot," the doctor said.

And that was the end of it. When he got up to go, no advice, no warning had been given.

"You're sure you're all right here?"

"Yes, of course," said Ramage.

"It's all rubbish," the doctor told his wife that evening. "The man's as fit as a fiddle, nothing wrong with him at all."

"Was Mrs. Ramage there?"

"No, thank God. She was out."

"I heard this morning," said Mrs. Cox, "that she's disappeared. Hasn't been seen for weeks."

The doctor laughed heartily. "Why can't they leave those two alone? What rubbish!"

"Well," said Mrs. Cox without smiling, "it's odd, isn't it?"

"Rubbish," the doctor said again some days later, for, spurred on by Mr. Eliot, people were talking venomously and he could not

stop them. Mrs. Ramage was not at Spanish
Castle, she was not in the town. Where was
she?

Old Myra was questioned. She said that
she had not seen her god-daughter and had
not heard from her 'since long time'. The Inspector of Police had two anonymous letters
—the first writer claimed to know 'all what
happen at Spanish Castle one night': the other
said that witnesses were frightened to come
forward and speak against a man.

The *Gazette* published a fiery article:

"The so-called 'Imperial Road' was meant
to attract young Englishmen with capital who
would buy and develop properties in the interior. This costly experiment has not been a
success, and one of the last of these gentle-
men planters has seen himself as the king of
the cannibal islands ever since he landed. We
have it, on the best authority, that his very
eccentric behaviour has been the greatest
possible annoyance to his neighbour. Now the
whole thing has become much more serious. . . ."

It ended: "Black people bear much; must
they also bear beastly murder and nothing
done about it?"

"You don't suppose that I believe all these
lies, do you?" Dr. Cox told Mr. Eliot, and Mr.
Eliot answered: "Then I'll make it my business to find out the truth. That man is a

menace, as I said from the first, and he should be dealt with."

"Dear Ramage," Dr. Cox wrote. "I'm sorry to tell you that stupid and harmful rumours are being spread about your wife and yourself. I need hardly say that no one with a grain of sense takes them seriously, but people here are excitable and very ready to believe mischiefmakers, so I strongly advise you to put a stop to the talk at once and to take legal action if necessary."

But the doctor got no answer to this letter, for in the morning news reached the town of a riot at Spanish Castle the night before.

A crowd of young men and boys, and a few women, had gone up to Ramage's house to throw stones. It was a bright moonlight night. He had come on to the verandah and stood there facing them. He was dressed in white and looked very tall, they said, like a zombi. He said something that nobody heard, a man had shouted "white zombi" and thrown a stone which hit him. He went into the house and came out with a shotgun. Then stories differed wildly. He had fired and hit a woman in the front of the crowd . . . No, he'd hit a little boy at the back . . . He hadn't fired at all, but had threatened them. It was agreed that in the rush to get away people had been knocked down and hurt, one woman seriously.

It was also rumoured that men and boys

from the village planned to burn down Spanish Castle house, if possible with Ramage inside. After this there was no more hesitation. The next day a procession walked up the garden path to the house—the Inspector of Police, three policemen and Dr. Cox.

"He must give some explanation of all this," said the Inspector.

The doors and windows were all open, and they found Ramage and the shotgun, but they got no explanation. He had been dead for some hours.

His funeral was an impressive sight. A good many came out of curiosity, a good many because, though his death was said to be "an accident", they felt guilty. For behind the coffin walked Mrs. Ramage, sent for post-haste by old Myra. She'd been staying with relatives in Guadeloupe. When asked why she had left so secretly—she had taken a fishing boat from the other side of the island—she answered sullenly that she didn't want anyone to know her business, she knew how people talked. No, she'd heard no rumours about her husband, and the *Gazette*—a paper written in English—was not read in Guadeloupe.

"Eh-eh," echoed Myra. "Since when the girl obliged to tell everybody where she go and what she do chapter and verse. . . ."

It was lovely weather, and on their way to

the Anglican cemetery many had tears in their eyes.

But already public opinion was turning against Ramage.

"His death was really a blessing in disguise," said one lady. "He was evidently mad, poor man—sitting in the sun with no clothes on—much worse might have happened."

"This is All Souls Day," Rosalie thought, standing at her bedroom window before going to sleep. She was wishing that Mr. Ramage could have been buried in the Catholic cemetery, where all day the candles burnt almost invisible in the sunlight. When night came they twinkled like fireflies. The graves were covered with flowers—some real, some red or yellow paper or little gold cut-outs. Sometimes there was a letter weighted by a stone and the black people said that next morning the letters had gone. And where? Who would steal letters on the night of the dead? But the letters had gone.

The Anglican cemetery, which was not very far away, down the hill, was deserted and silent. Protestants believed that when you were dead, you were dead.

If he had a letter . . . she thought.

"My dear darling Mr. Ramage," she wrote, then felt so sad that she began to cry.

Two hours later Mrs. Cox came into the room and found her daughter in bed and

asleep; on the table by her side was the un-
finished letter. Mrs. Cox read it, frowned,
pressed her lips together, then crumpled it
up and threw it out of the window.

There was a stiff breeze and she watched it
bouncing purposefully down the street. As if
it knew exactly where it was going.

Goodbye Marcus,
Goodbye Rose

"When first I wore my old shako," sang Captain Cardew, "Ten, twenty, thirty, forty, fifty years ago . . ." and Phoebe thought what a wonderful bass voice he had. This was the second time he had called to take her for a walk, and again he had brought her a large box of chocolates.

Captain Cardew and his wife were spending the winter in Jamaica when they visited the small island where she lived and found it so attractive and unspoilt that they decided to stay. They even talked of buying a house and settling there for good.

He was not only a very handsome old man but a hero who had fought bravely in some long ago war which she thought you only read about in history books. He'd been wounded and had a serious operation without an anaesthetic. Anaesthetics weren't invented in those days. (Better not think too much about that.)

23

It had been impressed on her how kind it
was of him to bother with a little girl like
herself. Anyway she liked him, he was always
so carefully polite to her, treating her as
though she were a grown-up girl. A calm un-
ruffled man, he only grew annoyed if people
called him "Captain" too often. Sometimes he
lost his temper and would say loudly things
like: "What d'you think I'm Captain of now
—a Penny a Liner?" What was a Penny a
Liner? She never found out.

It was a lovely afternoon and they set out.
She was wearing a white blouse with a sailor
collar, a long full white skirt, black stockings,
black buttoned boots and a large wide-
brimmed white hat anchored firmly with
elastic under her chin.

When they reached the Botanical Gardens
she offered to take him to a shady bench and
they walked slowly to the secluded part of
the Gardens that she'd spoken of and sat under a large tree. Beyond its shadow they could
see the yellow dancing patches of sunlight.

"Do you mind if I take off my hat? The
elastic is hurting me," Phoebe said.

"Then take it off, take it off," said the
Captain.

Phoebe took off her hat and began to talk
in what she hoped was a grown-up way about
the curator, Mr. Harcourt-Smith, who'd really
made the Gardens as beautiful as they were.

He'd come from a place in England called the Kew. Had he ever heard of it?

Yes he had heard of it. He added: "How old are you Phoebe?"

"I'm twelve," said Phoebe, "—and a bit."

"Hah!" said the Captain. "Then soon you'll be old enough to have a lover!" His hand, which had been lying quietly by his side, darted towards her, dived inside her blouse and clamped itself around one very small breast. "Quite old enough," he remarked.

Phoebe remained perfectly still. "He's making a great mistake, a great mistake," she thought. "If I don't move he'll take his hand away without really noticing what he's done."

However the Captain showned no sign of that at all. He was breathing rather heavily when a couple came strolling round the corner. Calmly, without hurry, he withdrew his hand and after a while said: "Perhaps we ought to be going home now."

Phoebe, who was in a ferment, said nothing. They walked out of the shade into the sun and as they walked she looked up at him as though at some aged but ageless god. He talked of usual things in a usual voice and she made up her mind that she would tell nobody of what had happened. Nobody. It was not a thing you could possibly talk about. Also no one would believe exactly how it had happened, and whether they believed her or not she would be blamed.

If he was as absentminded as all that—for surely it could be nothing but absentmindedness—perhaps there oughtn't to be any more walks. She could excuse herself by saying that she had a headache. But that would only do for once. The walks continued. They'd go into the Gardens or up the Morne, a hill overlooking the town. There were benches and seats there but few houses and hardly anybody about.

He never touched her again but all through the long bright afternoons Captain Cardew talked of love and Phoebe listened, shocked and fascinated. Sometimes she doubted what he said: surely it was impossible, horrifyingly impossible. Sometimes she was on the point of saying, not "You oughtn't to talk to me like this" but babyishly "I want to go home". He always knew when she felt this and would at once change the subject and tell her amusing stories of his life when he was a young man and a subaltern in India.

"Hot?" he'd say. "This isn't hot. India's hot. Sometimes the only thing to do is take off your clothes and see that the punkah's going."

Or he'd talk about London long ago. Someone—was it Byron?—had said that women were never so unattractive as when they were eating and it was still most unfashionable for them to eat heartily. He'd watch in wonder as the ethereal creatures pecked daintily, then sent away almost untouched plates. One day he had seen a maid taking a tray laden with food up to the bedrooms and the mystery was explained.

But these stories were only intervals in the ceaseless talk of love, various ways of making love, various sorts of love. He'd explain that love was not kind and gentle, as she had imagined, but violent. Violence, even cruelty, was an essential part of it. He would expand on this, it seemed to be his favourite subject.

The walks had gone on for some time when the Captain's wife, Edith, who was a good deal younger than her husband, became suspicious and began making very sarcastic remarks. Early one evening when the entire party had gone up the Morne to watch the sunset, she'd said to her husband, after a long look at Phoebe: "Do you really find the game worth the candle?" Captain Cardew said nothing. He watched the sun going down without expression, then remarked that it was quite true that the only way to get rid of a temptation was to yield to it.

Phoebe had never liked Edith very much. Now she began to dislike her. One afternoon they were in a room together and she said: "Do you see how white my hair's becoming? It's all because of you." And when Phoebe answered truthfully that she didn't notice any white hairs: "What a really dreadful little liar you are!"

After this she must have spoken to Phoebe's

mother, a silent, reserved woman, who said
nothing to her daughter but began to watch
her in a puzzled, incredulous, even faintly
suspicious way. Phoebe knew that very soon
she would be questioned, she'd have to explain.

So she was more than half relieved when
Edith Cardew announced that they'd quite
given up their first idea of spending the rest
of the winter on the island and were going
back to England by the next boat. When
Captain Cardew said "Goodbye" formally,
the evening before they left, she had smiled
and shaken hands, not quite realizing that
she was very unlikely ever to see him again.

There was a flat roof outside her bedroom
window. On hot fine nights she'd often lie
there in her nightgown looking up at the
huge brilliant stars. She'd once tried to write
a poem about them but had not got beyond
the first line: "My stars. Familiar jewels." But
that night she knew that she would never finish it. They were not jewels. They were not
familiar. They were cold, infinitely far away,
quite indifferent.

The roof looked onto the yard and she could
hear Victoria and Joseph talking and laughing outside the pantry, then they must have
gone away and it was quite silent. She was
alone in the house for she'd not gone with
the others to see the Cardews off. She was

sure that now they had gone her mother
would be very unlikely to question her, and
then began to wonder how he had been so
sure, not only that she'd never tell anybody
but that she'd make no effort at all to stop
him talking. That could only mean that he'd
seen at once that she was not a good girl—
who would object—but a wicked one—who
would listen. He must know. He knew. It was
so.

It was so and she felt not so much unhappy
about this as uncomfortable, even dismayed.
It was like wearing a dress that was much
too big for her, a dress that swallowed her up.

Wasn't it quite difficult being a wicked
girl? Even more difficult than being a good
one? Besides, didn't the nuns say that Chastity, in Thought, Word and Deed was your
most precious possession? She remembered
Mother Sacred Heart, her second favourite,
reciting in her lovely English voice:

"So *dear to Heaven is saintly chastity. . . .*"
How did it go on? Something about "*a thousand liveried angels lackey her. . . .*"

"A thousand liveried angels" now no more.
The thought of some vague irreparable loss
saddened her. Then she told herself that anyway she needn't bother any longer about
whether she'd get married or not. The older
girls that she knew talked a great deal about
marriage, some of them talked about very
little else. And they seemed so sure. No

sooner had they put their hair up and begun going to dances, than they'd marry someone handsome (and rich). Then the fun of being grown-up and important, of doing what you wanted instead of what you were told to do, would start. And go on for a long long time.

But she'd always doubted if this would happen to her. Even if numbers of rich and handsome young men suddenly appeared, would she be one of the chosen?

> *If no one ever marries me*
> *And I don't see why they should*
> *For nurse says I'm not pretty*
> *And I'm seldom very good . . .*

That was it exactly.

Well there was one thing. Now she felt very wise, very grown-up, she could forget these childish worries. She could hardly believe that only a few weeks ago she, like all the others, had secretly made lists of her trousseau, decided on the names of her three children. Jack. Marcus. And Rose.

Now goodbye Marcus. Goodbye Rose. The prospect before her might be difficult and uncertain but it was far more exciting.

The Bishop's Feast

When I'd left Dominica twenty-five years ago there were no hotels, only a small boarding-house run by three sisters. The few people who wished to stay usually rented a house. So I was relieved when I saw the large cool room in the La Paz. There was a bathroom, and flush lavatories. All was well.

The next morning one of my mother's old friends sent me some flowers, and there was a letter from Mother Mount Calvary, the Mother Superior of the convent where I was at school, whom I had loved so much. She wrote "Welcome back to Dominica. Come to see us at 4 o'clock this afternoon. How could I forget you?"

I asked the driver of the car we had hired to take me to the convent. He told me the old convent I knew had been sold, and the nuns were now living in a much smaller building. They would soon be going back to England and would be replaced by nuns of a Belgian order. "I hear the old nun says she won't go, but she'll soon find out that she has to."

"Isn't it rather a shame," I said, "to make them leave when they've worked so hard here, all their lives?"

He said "They're too old for the job, anyway."

Mother Mount Calvary—Good Mother, we used to call her—was smiling when she welcomed me and looked almost as cheerful as I remembered her. When she stopped smiling I saw that her face was very sombre and old. We sat in the garden with two other nuns who I thought I didn't know. One of them remarked how much I had changed.

"She hasn't changed at all," Mother Mount Calvary said sharply.

When I looked again at the nun I recognized something in her expression. She was the little Irish nun I had once seen smiling at her reflection in a barrel of water. There were no dimples now. She was a frightened old lady.

So this was the end of the feud between the convent and the bishopric, which had started at the new bishop's feast.

We'd all subscribed towards a present for the new bishop. It was an armchair to be given to him when he came to watch the performance celebrating his feast. We were excited about this performance.

The evening came. We clustered in the wings listening to a girl reciting *"Partant pour la Syrie"*, which was the first item on the programme. She didn't seem at all nervous. Her voice sounded clear and assured:

*"Partant pour la Syrie le jeune et beau Dunois
Venait prier Marie de bénir ses exploits.
'Faites, Reine Immortelle,' lui dit-il en partant,
'Que j'aime la plus belle et sois le plus vaillant.'"*

Louise was dressed for her song *"L'Anglaise à Paris"*, a mild satire on Englishwomen in Paris and the next item, when Mother St. Edmund came bustling in and without giving us any reason told us that the programme had been changed. *"L'Anglaise à Paris"* was cancelled, instead a selected chorus was to sing "Killarney".

Consternation, giggles.

"Don't be silly, children," said Mother St. Edmund. "Sing up and do your best. You all know the words."

"He won't like that one either," said Mother Sacred Heart. But Mother St. Edmund urged us on:

*"By Killarney's lakes and fells,
Emerald isles and winding bays. . . ."*

From the stage we could see the bishop enthroned in his new armchair, Mother Mount Calvary by his side. A large audience of parents and friends stretched away to the end of the room.

". . . *Beauty's home, Killarney,*
Heaven's reflex, Killarney."

The curtain came down.

Somebody played a Chopin mazurka and everything went more or less smoothly on to a series of tableaux vivants, the most important part of the programme.

The first one was of the Last Supper with Mary Magdalene at the feet of Christ. None of the apostles appeared. Delia Paulson's hair was exactly right—she played Mary Magdalene—though her face, which was hidden, wouldn't have done at all. Mildred Watts was Jesus Christ. She was lovely, just like Jesus. The nuns had fixed her up with a little beard and she looked into the distance over Mary's head. (I thought Christ might have looked at Mary but I suppose the nuns told Mildred not to.) However, His hand was raised in a rather absentminded blessing.

The next tableau was the Death of St. Cecilia, patron saint of music. There was a statue of her above the piano on which I practised and I always thought she looked at me most severely when I played the waltzes of Rodolphe Berger instead of my scales. St. Cecilia lay smiling on a couch with one finger over three to symbolize that she believed in the Three in One.

So the tableaux went on and we peeped at the bishop, but he didn't applaud. The old bishop always clapped loudly and smiled, but this bishop seemed very bored.

When the programme ended we trooped onto the stage to hear the bishop give his little speech of thanks and appreciation. There was a pause, because for some reason he didn't seem able to get up. He put his hands on the arms of the chair, turned round, glared and tried again. No use.

Soon it was plain what happened; he had stuck to the chair, which had been taken to be varnished and the varnish hadn't quite dried. Some of the nuns looked apprehensive and hurried to help him, but Mother Superior, who dearly loved a joke, couldn't stop herself from smiling broadly. Just as she smiled the bishop looked straight at her, their eyes met, she suppressed the smile, but it was too late.

Soon afterwards he came to the school to give us dictation. I liked the colour of his purple skull cap but I hated his face. The old bishop had a light voice, he had a heavy throaty voice. He dictated: "I have a dog. His name is Toby. He can bark and he can bite . . ."

That's how it began. He started trying to get rid of them even before I left the island.

Of course Mother Mount Calvary had her friends and must have fought back, but even she couldn't fight old age. It was a sad meeting. When I left them I promised to visit them again before they sailed.

But I never saw them again. I went away to spend a week on the Atlantic side of the island, and when I returned to the town the day before they were to leave, I was told that Mother Mount Calvary had died that morning. I felt very sad, but also something like triumph, because in the end she had won. She had always done what she said she'd do. She had said she would never leave the island, and she hadn't.

Heat

Ash had fallen. Perhaps it had fallen the night before or perhaps it was still falling. I can only remember in patches. I was looking at it two feet deep on the flat roof outside my bedroom. The ash and the silence. Nobody talked in the street, nobody talked while we ate, or hardly at all. I know now that they were all frightened. They thought our volcano was going up.

Our volcano was called the boiling lake. That's what it was, a sheet of water that always boiled. From what fires? I thought of it as a mysterious place that few people had ever seen. In the churchyard where we often went—for death was not then a taboo subject —quite near the grave of my little sister, was a large marble headstone. "Sacred to the memory of Clive ———, who lost his life at the boiling lake in Dominica in an heroic attempt to save his guide". Aged twenty-seven. I remember that too.

He was a young Englishman, a visitor, who had gone exploring with two guides to the boiling lake. As they were standing looking at it one of the guides, who was a long way ahead, staggered and fell. The other seized hold of the Englishman's hand and said "Run!" There must have been some local tradition that poisonous gases sometimes came out of the lake. After a few steps the Englishman pulled his hand away and went back and lifted up the man who had fallen. Then he too staggered and they both fell. The surviving guide ran and told what had happened.

In the afternoon two little friends were coming to see us and to my surprise they both arrived carrying large glass bottles. Both the bottles had carefully written labels pasted on: "Ash collected from the streets of Roseau on May 8th, 1902." The little boy asked me if I'd like to have his jar, but I refused. I didn't want to touch the ash. I don't remember the rest of the day. I must have gone to bed, for that night my mother woke me and without saying anything, led me to the window. There was a huge black cloud over Martinique. I couldn't ever describe that cloud, so huge and black it was, but I have never forgotten it. There was no moon, no stars, but the edges of the cloud were flame-coloured and in the middle what looked to me like lightning flickered, never stopping.

My mother said: "You will never see anything like this in your life again." That was all. I must have gone to sleep at the window and been carried to bed.

Next morning we heard what had happened. Was it a blue or a grey day? I only know ash wasn't falling any longer. The Roseau fishermen went out very early, as they did in those days. They met the fishermen from Port de France, who knew. That was how we heard before the cablegrams, the papers and all the rest came flooding in. That was how we heard of Mont Pelée's eruption and the deaths of 40,000 people, and that there was nothing left of St. Pierre.

As soon as ships were sailing again between Dominica and Martinique my father went to see the desolation that was left. He brought back a pair of candlesticks, tall heavy brass candlesticks which must have been in a church. The heat had twisted them into an extraordinary shape. He hung them on the wall of the dining-room and I stared at them all through meals, trying to make sense of the shape.

It was after this that the gossip started. That went on for years so I can remember it well. St. Pierre, they said, was a very wicked city. It had not only a theatre, but an opera house, which was probably wickeder still. Companies from Paris performed there. But worse than this was the behaviour of the

women who were the prettiest in the West
Indies. They tied their turbans in a particular
way, a sort of language of love that all St.
Pierre people understood. Tied in one way it
meant "I am in love, I am not free"; tied in
another way it meant "You are welcome, I
am free". Even the women who were married,
or as good as, tied their kerchiefs in the "I am
free" way. And that wasn't all. The last bishop
who had visited the city had taken off his
shoes and solemnly shaken them over it. After
that, of course, you couldn't wonder.

As I grew older I heard of a book by a
man called Lafcadio Hearn who had written
about St. Pierre as it used to be, about Ti
Marie and all the others but I never found
the book and stopped looking for it. However, one day I did discover a pile of old
newspapers and magazines, some illustrated:
the English version of the eruption. They
said nothing about the opera house or the
theatre which must have seemed to the English the height of frivolity in a Caribbean
island, and very little about the city and its
inhabitants. It was nearly all about the one
man who had survived. He was a convict im-
prisoned in an underground cell, so he
escaped—the only one out of 40,000. He was
now travelling round the music-halls of the
world being exhibited. They had taught him
a little speech. He must be quite a rich man
—what did he do with his money? Would

he marry again? His wife and children had been killed in the eruption. . . . I read all this, then I thought but it wasn't like that, it wasn't like that at all.

Fishy Waters

THE EDITOR
The Dominica Herald   March 3rd, 189–

Dear Sir,

Yesterday I heard a piece of news that appalled me. It seems that a British workman, Mr. Longa by name, who arrived a year ago, has been arrested and is being held by the police. Mr. Longa is a carpenter. He is also a socialist, and does not disguise his political opinions. It goes without saying that a certain class of person in this island, who seem to imagine that the colour of their skins enables them to behave like gods, disliked and disapproved of him from the first. He was turned out of Miss Lambton's boarding-house after one night and had the greatest difficulty in finding anywhere to live. Eventually he settled in a predominantly negro quarter—another cause for offence. A determined effort was made to induce him to leave the island. When this failed, with their usual hypocrisy they pretended to ignore him, but they were merely biding their time.

He was found joking roughly with one of the many vagabond children who infest the streets of Roseau, and is to be accused of child-molesting and cruelty, if you please. A trumped-up charge, on the face of it. In this way, they plan to be rid of a long-standing nuisance and to be able to boast about their even-handed justice. The hypocrisy of these people, who bitterly resent that they no longer have the power over the bodies and minds of the blacks they once had (the cruelty of West Indian planters was a by-word), making a scape-goat of an honest British workman, is enough to make any decent person's gorge rise. A London barrister, new to this island, has offered to defend Mr. Longa without charge. Only one just man among so many?

> Yours truly,
> Disgusted

THE EDITOR
The Dominica Herald   March 10, 189–

Dear Sir,

Who is "Disgusted"? Who is this person (I believe people) who tries to stir up racial hatred whenever possible? Almost invariably with gloating satisfaction, they will drag in the horrors of the slave trade. Who would think, to hear them talk, that slavery was abolished by the English nearly a hundred years ago? They are long on diatribes, but short on facts. The slave trade was an abominable one, but it could not have existed without the help and cooperation of African chiefs. Slavery still exists, and is taken for granted, in Africa, both among Negroes and Arabs. Are these facts ever mentioned? The bad is endlessly repeated and insisted upon; the good is ridiculed, forgotten or denied. Who does this, and why?

Yours truly,
Ian J. MacDonald

THE EDITOR
The Dominica Herald   March 17th, 189–

Dear Sir,

It is sometimes said that African chiefs probably had a good deal to do with the slave trade, but I have never heard before that this was proven. In his typical letter I notice that Mr. MacDonald places all the blame on these perhaps mythical Africans and says nothing about the greed of white merchants or the abominable cruelty and indifference of white planters. The treatment meted out to Mr. Longa shows that their heirs and successors have not changed all that much.

Yours truly,
P. Kelly
Kelly's Universal Stores

THE EDITOR
The Dominica Herald   March 24th, 189–

Dear Sir,

I hate to interfere with the amusement of your readers, but I must point out that according to English law it is highly improper to discuss a case that has not been tried (*sub judice*). In this country the custom seems to be more honoured in the breach than in the observance.

Yours truly,
Fiat Justicia

This correspondence is now closed. *Editor*.

On the same day the editor, who was known as Papa Dom, remarked in a leading article: "These are fishy waters—very fishy waters."

*   *   *

6 Cork Street
Roseau, Dominica   March 24th, 189–

My dear Caroline,

Your letter rescued me from a mood of great depression. I am answering it at once—it will be such a relief to tell you about something that I don't care to discuss with people here.

You wouldn't remember a man called

Jimmy Longa—he arrived soon after you left. Well, Matt found him trying to saw a little girl in two—can you believe it?—and is to be the main witness for the prosecution. The whole place is buzzing with gossip, arguments, letters to the local newspaper and so on. It is most unpleasant. I've begged Matt to have nothing further to do with it, I'm sure there'll be trouble. He says why should there be, Longa's a white man not a black one. I say "Jimmy Longa will be an honorary black before this is over, you'll see. They'll twist it somehow." But he won't even talk about it now. I'm not at all happy about Matt. He doesn't look well and is so unlike what he used to be. I begin to wish I'd never persuaded him to settle here when he retired—a visit to escape the winter is one thing, living here is quite another.

The first scandal about Longa was that Miss Lambton turned him out as he got so drunk every night. He's a jobbing carpenter, quite a good one when he's sober, so he soon found a place to live and got plenty of work. His story is that he's on his way to America and stopped off at Dominica to make some money. I wonder who on earth could have advised him to do that! He gave out that he was a socialist, extreme—the new world must be built on the ashes of the old, that sort of thing. He preached fire and slaughter in the rum-shop and everywhere else so you can imagine he wasn't very popular with the white people. Then he got malaria badly and Miss Lambton, who had him on her conscience, went to the hospital to see how he was. She said he looked very ill and told her that his only wish now was to get back to England, but he couldn't raise the money. She started a subscription for him and headed the list with £10, which she certainly couldn't afford. Nearly everyone chipped in and a good deal was raised. But somehow he managed to persuade Miss Lambton to hand the lot over directly. Then disappeared. There was no case against him—he'd been careful not to promise or sign anything—besides, a lot of people thought it comic. They said "Poor Mamie Lambton, it seems she's very upset. But what a chap! You have to laugh!" Even when he reappeared, more fanatical than ever, nobody took him seriously—he was the Dominica funny story. And now this.

I've got one piece of pleasant news. Because Matt dislikes the town so much we've bought a small estate in the country where he may be happier. It's called Three Rivers—an old place, and as usual the house is falling to bits. It's being fixed up—but lately I've wondered if we'll ever live there.

No one at home would understand why all this is looming over me so much, but you know the kind of atmosphere we get here sometimes, so I think you will.

I'm so glad you are happy and don't feel the cold too much. Perhaps the next time I write it will all be over and I'll be more cheerful.

> Meanwhile I send you my love,
> Affectionately,
> Maggie

      ❀   ❀   ❀

The day after Jimmy Longa's trial there was a long report on the front page of the *Dominica Herald*. The reporter, having remarked on the crowded court-room, usually empty for assault and battery cases, went on to say that the prosecuting counsel, M. Didier of Roseau, had seemed so nervous at first that he was almost inaudible. His speech was short. He said that it was fortunate that there had been an eye-witness to the attack on the child, Josephine Mary Dent, known as Jojo, for though Mr. Longa's activities were common knowledge in Roseau, no one had dared to come forward to accuse him, a white man. "There are a certain number of children, abandoned and unprotected, roaming the streets. This child was one of them. The accused is a danger to all children, but these are particularly at risk." M. Didier asked for a sentence heavy enough to deter possible imitators. He then called his first witness, Mr. Matthew Penrice.

Mr. Penrice said that on the late afternoon of February 27th he was walking up Jetty Street on the way to the Club when he heard a child screaming in a very distressing way. As he approached the house the screams came from, the sound stopped abruptly—no angry voices, complete silence. The house stood well back from the empty street, and there was a fence round it. It occurred to him that a child, left alone there, might have met with an accident, and on an impulse he knocked at the wooden gate. There was no answer so he pushed the gate open. As he did so he heard a man say: "Now I'm going to saw you in two, like they do in English music halls." The yard of the house was quite a large one; there was a tree in the corner, and under the tree a plank raised up on trestles. A naked little negro girl lay on the plank, her head hanging over the end. She was silent, and her face was almost green with fright. The man's back was to him and the saw in his hand was touching the child's waist. Mr. Penrice called out "What the devil's going on here?" The man turned, dropping the saw, and he recognized Mr. Longa, who was not in court. Mr. Longa said: "I wasn't going to hurt her—I was only joking." He had been holding the child on the plank, and when he turned she rolled off and lay on the ground without moving. Mr. Longa repeated that it was a joke. When the witness approached the unconscious child he saw that her body was covered with bruises. He did not speak to Mr. Longa again, but wrapped the child in his jacket and took her to the house of Madame Octavia Joseph, which was close by. He then sent for the doctor who fortunately was able to come at once. After the doctor had arrived he went to the police station and reported what he had seen.

Cross-examined by counsel for the defence, Mr. Penrice was asked if Jetty Street was his usual way to the Club. He answered that it was not, but he was in a hurry to keep an appointment and Jetty Street was a short cut.

Counsel asked him: "Would it surprise you to know that information from your household reveals that on that particular day you left for the Club very much earlier than usual? The domestic remembers it clearly, as it was her birthday. As your habits are so regular, she wondered why you had left the house on foot on such a hot day, nearly two hours earlier than usual. Why, then, did you have to take a short cut?"

Mr. Penrice replied: "Two hours is an exaggeration. I left my house earlier than usual to go for a walk—I don't mind the heat—and I forgot the time, so I was trying to get to the Club as quickly as I could."

"When you heard the accused say 'Like they do in English music halls', was he aware that anyone was listening?"

"No, he didn't know that I was there."

"So he was speaking to the child?"

"I suppose so."

"Do you know that there is a popular trick on the English music halls when a girl is supposed to be sawn in two?"

"Yes, I think so."

"And is anyone ever sawn in two, or hurt in any way?"

"Of course not. It's a trick."

"Perhaps you were too startled and shocked to realize that when the accused said 'As they do in English music halls' he was really declaring that what he was about to do was not to be taken seriously. It was a joke."

"It was not a joke."

"And why are you so sure of that?"

"When the man faced me, I knew that it was not a joke at all."

"I see. But is there not a certain amount of prejudice against Mr. Longa in this island? Are you not very ready to believe the worst of him? Has there not been a great deal of gossip about him?"

"I only know Mr. Longa by sight. The gossip here does not interest me."

"So you are not—shall we say—prejudiced?"

"No, not at all. Not in the way you mean."

"I am glad to hear it. Now, as you say the child was unconscious and badly hurt, would not the normal thing have been either to take or to send her to the hospital?"

"I didn't think of the hospital. Madame Joseph's house was nearby and I knew she would be well looked-after so I took her there and sent for the doctor."

"Mr. Penrice, has Madame Joseph ever been in your service?"

"Yes. She was with us for nearly five years, off and on, when we used to winter here before making it our home. That was why I was so sure that she was not only a kind woman, but a perfectly reliable one."

"When she left your employment, did you give her a large present of money?"

"Not large, no. Both my wife and myself thought she had given us invaluable service. She was no longer in very good health, so we were happy to give her enough to buy a small house, where she would be comfortable and secure."

"No doubt she was very grateful?"

"I think she was pleased, yes."

"As she was so indebted to you, you must have been sure that in an emergency any instructions you gave her would be carried out?"

"In saying that, you only show that you know nothing at all about the people of this island. Madame Joseph is a most independent woman. Even if I—or rather, we—had installed her in a palace instead of a small house, she would not have thought herself bound to follow my instructions. No."

"And it really seemed to you proper to leave a badly injured child in the care of an ex-servant, however devoted, who had no medical knowledge and no experience of nursing?"

"I did what I thought best for her."

"And did you tell the doctor that you had taken her there because Madame Joseph was the child's close relative?"

"I did nothing of the sort."

"But you can imply a thing without actually saying it, can you not?"

"You most certainly can."

"Thank you, Mr. Penrice. You may stand down."

Mr. Penrice was followed in the witness box by Madame Octavia Joseph, a dignified woman who gave her evidence clearly and obviously made a favourable impression on the magistrate, Mr. Somers. When she saw the state the little girl was in, she said, she understood why Mr. Penrice was going to the police. "It was a very wicked person did that." Soon after the doctor came the child recovered consciousness, but at once began to tremble and scream. Having treated her bruises, the doctor gave her a sedative, said he would call next day, that she was to see nobody, and that she was not to be questioned until she was better. Madame Joseph had done her best to follow the doctor's orders and had taken great care of the child, whose condition was much improved; "But she says she does not remember anything about being attacked. When I told her she ought to try to remember, she only began to cry and shake, so I thought it better for the doctor to speak to her."

The last witness for the prosecution, Dr. Trevor, said that on the evening of February 27th he had been at home when he got a message to come at once to 11 Hill Street to treat a badly injured child. When he first saw the child she had fainted and obviously been savagely beaten. When she recovered consciousness she was so frightened and hysterical that after treating her he gave her a sedative. She was probably about eleven or twelve years of age, but as she was very thin and undernourished, she may have been a year or two older.

Counsel asked Dr. Trevor: "Have you seen the child since?"

"Yes, on several occasions."

"When did you see her last?"

"I saw her yesterday."

"And what did you think of her?"

"I found that her condition had greatly improved. She has been carefully looked after and is well on the way to recovery. Already she seems quite a different child."

"When you visited this child, did you ever

question her or ask her who had attacked her?"

"Yes, after I thought she was better I did question her, of course. She always behaved in the same way. She says she has forgotten. I tried two or three times to question her more closely—the only result is that she becomes frightened, hysterical and quite incoherent."

"When you questioned the child, was Madame Joseph with you?"

"She was there the first time, but I have often been alone with the child and this is invariably the way she behaves."

"Did it strike you at all that because of what has happened, she had been mentally affected?"

"No, I saw no signs of that. She'd probably be quite a bright little thing, given a chance."

"Did you not think it somewhat strange that although she is so much better, she still refuses to say anything about what happened to her?"

"Perhaps it is not as strange as you think. Some people after a great shock or fright will talk volubly, others 'clam up' as they say in parts of England. She'll probably talk eventually, but it's impossible to say when."

"And you find nothing unusual about this 'clamming up', as you call it?"

"I have known cases when, after a frightening and harmful experience, the mind has protected itself by forgetting. If you try to force recollection, the patient becomes agitated and resentful."

"Do you really think that this interesting but rather complicated theory could apply to a Negro child, completely illiterate, only eleven or twelve years of age? Is it not more likely that she remains silent because she has either been persuaded or threatened—probably a bit of both—not to talk?"

"I do not believe that the result of illiteracy is an uncomplicated mind—far from it. And I do not know who you are suggesting could have frightened her. My orders were that she should be kept perfectly quiet and see no one except Madame Joseph, whose house is surrounded by inquisitive neighbours. If anyone else had been there I would have been told, believe me. The child certainly isn't at all afraid of Madame Joseph. On the contrary, she seems to trust her, even be attached to her—insofar as a child like that can trust or be attached at all. However, if you are not satisfied with my evidence, why not question the child? In my opinion you will get nothing at all out of her and may do her harm, but you must decide for yourself."

Here Mr. Somers intervened and said that the child must certainly not be questioned by anyone as long as the doctor thought it might be harmful.

Counsel then asked Dr. Trevor: "Were you

led to believe that the child had been taken to Madame Joseph's house because she was a close relative?"

"No. I suppose I took it for granted. In any case, I made no suggestion that she should be moved. I thought she was in very good hands."

Counsel for the Defence, Mr. Berkeley, said that his client was too ill to appear in Court, but that he would read his statement. This, he submitted, was a complete answer to the charge.

Mr. Longa's Statement: "I had not felt very well that day. It was too hot, so I thought I'd knock off for a bit. But as I might be able to work later on when it was cooler, I left my saw in the yard, with a plank I was working on to make bookshelves. I was very thirsty and had a few drinks, then I fell asleep. I don't know how long I slept before loud screams woke me up, coming from my yard. The noise these children make is very trying and that's putting it mildly. They climb over the fence into the yard to play, and get up to all kinds of mischief. I'd chase them away, but they always came back. They'd follow me in the street, jeering and laughing, and several times I've been stoned. I don't deny I've grown to dislike them very much indeed.

"I got up feeling shaky and in a bad temper, and in my yard I found a little girl lying

on the ground, screaming. I asked her what
was the matter several times, but she took no
notice at all and went on yelling. At last I
told her to shut up, get out, and go and
scream somewhere else. She wouldn't even
look at me, and the noise she was making
went through and through my head, so I lost
my temper, picked her up and put her on
the plank, telling her I was going to saw her
in two, but I didn't really mean to hurt her
and I told her so. I didn't notice anything
wrong with her, or think it strange that she
was naked—they very often are, especially
on hot days. No, I never meant to hurt her.
But I hoped to frighten her a bit, and that
she'd tell the others, and then perhaps they'd
leave me in peace. These children had made
my life a misery, and I wanted to stop them
from doing it. I swear that was all I meant—
to frighten her. It was just a joke. When Mr.
Penrice came and accused me I was too confused to say much. I told him I hadn't meant
any harm but he wouldn't listen to me, nor
would the policemen when they arrested me.
I am sorry for what I did and for frightening
her, but I had been drinking. I quite lost my
temper and was very angry. That is what
happened, and that is the truth."

To this Mr. Berkeley added that Mr. Longa
was now very willing to leave the island. "He
says that even in England he would not be
treated with such injustice. As to the rumours

about my client, I am surprised that my learned friend has mentioned them, as he has failed to produce a single witness to substantiate them. Without wishing to impugn Mr. Penrice's word, I must point out that there is no evidence at all that Mr. Longa was the child's attacker. She may have run into the empty yard to hide, or—more likely —she was thrown there by the real attacker who then made off, feeling certain that Mr. Longa would be accused. Mr. Penrice admits that he heard Mr. Longa saying 'As they do in English music halls' before he knew anyone was listening. This seems to me to prove conclusively that Mr. Longa's behaviour was a joke—a rough, even a cruel joke if you like, but certainly not deserving of several years imprisonment in a gaol not fit for any human being, Englishman or not."

Mr. Berkeley ended by saying that Mr. Longa was a very intelligent man left terribly alone and isolated—also he was not a well man. It was hardly surprising that he turned to rum for consolation, and easy to believe that, woken suddenly, he felt extremely irritable and behaved in a way that was not normal to him.

The Summing-up. The magistrate, Mr. Somers, said that this was a very disturbing case. "There is no direct evidence that it was Mr. Longa who first attacked the child, causing the extensive bruising. He denies it strongly, and the child cannot yet be questioned. I find his statement as read by Counsel for the Defence convincing up to a point. Two things, however, strike me as unlikely. Why should he think that this unfortunate child would know anything about English music halls or the tricks performed there? Why should his mentioning them reassure her? It probably added to her fright. Also, and more important: however drunk he was, could he have picked up a badly injured naked child and carried her to the plank without noticing the marks on her body? According to Mr. Longa he noticed nothing, but proceeded with his savage joke. I find this so unlikely as to be almost incredible. He excuses himself by saying that he had been drinking, but he is a man accustomed to strong drink and there is no report of advanced intoxication from the police who arrested him.

"I am not here to speculate and I cannot accept either hearsay evidence or innuendoes supported by no evidence; but I have not been in my post for twenty years without learning that it is extremely difficult to obtain direct evidence here. Often a criminal is quite well-known, but the police find it impossible to produce a single witness against him. There is, unfortunately, in these islands a great distrust both of the police and of the law."

Here a voice interrupted: "Can you blame them?" and there was hubbub in the Court. Several women were in tears. Order was only restored when a threat was made to clear the Court.

Mr. Somers continued: "We can only hope that this perhaps natural distrust will diminish with time. In view of my doubts I am glad to hear that Mr. Longa is willing to leave the island. I direct that his passage to Southampton be paid by the Government. Until he sails he must remain in custody of the police, but must be allowed to receive visitors. He must be able to get food or provisions from outside and care must be taken to restore him to health. I am sure that his able Counsel will see that my instructions are carried out."

The crowd was subdued and less talkative than usual as it left the court-room, but a group of rowdies shouted at Mr. Penrice as he came out. He took no notice of this demonstration, but got into his waiting trap and drove off. A few stones were thrown after him, but the rowdies quickly dispersed when a policeman intervened.

"I bet you anything Mamie Lambton's going to start another subscription," said Matthew Penrice to his wife when he got home. He added: "Don't look so gloomy, Maggie. I've one piece of very good news. Octavia tells me that she's been corresponding with an old friend in St. Lucia with no children of her own who wishes to adopt Jojo. She's quite sure of this woman and says it'll be the best thing possible. I think so too. She'd get right away from all the gossip and questioning here, and start again. I'll see to it that she gets there as soon as she's well enough. I'll take care of everything, don't worry."

*　　*　　*

Maggie Penrice watched the Negro maid Janet pile the coffee things onto the tray and walk out, silent, barefooted. When she had said "What delicious coffee, Janet," the girl hadn't answered, hadn't even smiled. But they don't smile here, they laugh, they seldom smile. Not smilers with a knife. No? Even when they were alone she didn't speak, but went on folding and unfolding the letter. She re-read the last paragraph.

"Thank you for the money you sent. I will keep it faithfully and carefully for her when she grows up and thank you from my heart for giving her to me. You would be pleased to see her. She is getting quite fat and pretty and hardly ever wakes up screaming as she used to do. I now close and say no more from my over-flowing heart. Wishing you and your amiable lady all health and prosperity. Annie Dib."

Maggie said: "Dib. What a funny name."

"Syrian, probably," Matt said. "Well, that's the last of that, I hope, and now you mustn't worry any more. Much the best thing that could have happened. Surely you agree?"

"Perhaps. . . . But Matt, do you think it was wise to send her away quite so quickly?"

"The sooner the better, I should have thought. Why not?"

The room was at the back of the house, there was no noise from the street. It was hot and airless and the blinds were half drawn. She folded the letter carefully and put it back into its envelope, then pushed it across to him.

"Because it's all over the place that Octavia's in your pay and that you both sent the child to St. Lucia so that there was no chance of her ever talking. They're saying that you did it and pushed it off onto Jimmy Longa. The whole thing is utterly ridiculous, of course, but you ought to stop it."

"Stop it? What do you want me to do? How can I stop it?"

"Surely that wouldn't be too hard. It's so absurd. How could you have done it—how is it even possible?"

"Do you think these damnable hogs care whether it's possible or not, or how or where or when? They've just got hold of something to grunt about, that's all. If you think I'm going to argue with this lot you must be mad.

I've had more than enough of this whole damned place. If you really want to know what I feel, I want to clear out. It's not this particular storm in a tea-cup that's decided me. I've wanted to leave for some time, and you must have known it."

"They'll say you've run away."

"God, can't you get it into your head that I don't give a damn what they say here? Oh come on, Maggie, don't look like that. I know how you feel, how you dread the cold, how much better you are here, and its beauty and all that—I only wish I felt like you, but to me it's suffocating."

"Yes, I know. But I hoped you'd feel better when we left Roseau."

"The hatred would be exactly the same in the country—suppressed, perhaps. If you don't want to leave you needn't. I won't sell Three Rivers or this house, and the money will be all right—surely you know that?"

"But Matt, you find envy, malice, hatred everywhere. You can't escape."

"Perhaps, but I'm sick of this particular brand."

"Do you think I'd want to stay here by myself if you went? Do you really think that?"

He didn't answer but smiled and said: "Then that's settled." He patted her shoulder lightly, then he went over to an armchair, took up a book; but Maggie, watching him

anxiously, cautiously, saw that he never
turned a page. Suddenly she screwed up her
eyes tightly and shook her head. She was
trying to fight the overwhelming certainty
that the man she was looking at was a complete stranger.

Overture and
Beginners Please

We were sitting by the fire in the small
dining-room when Camilla said "I hate my
parents, don't you?" Hail was rattling against
the curtained windows. I had been told all
about snow long before I left the West Indies,
hail was a surprise and exciting in its way.
I thought I'd be laughed at if I asked what
it was.

Another dark yellow curtain hung over the
door which led into a passage and beyond
that were the empty classrooms, for this was
the week after Christmas and the day girls
and other seven boarders had gone home for
their holidays.

"And what's more," said Camilla, "they hate
me. They like my younger sister. A lot of
that sort of thing goes on in families but it's
hushed up of course."

It was almost dark, I was almost warm, so
I said, "I don't hate mine. They gave a fare-
well dance for me before I left. We had a

band. It's funny, I can remember exactly the face of the man with the shak-shak."

"How comic," said Camilla who seemed annoyed.

"They play well. Different music of course."

"Why did they send you to the old Perse if they were so fond of you?"

"Because my English aunt said it was a good school."

"That's the one who won't have you with her for Christmas, isn't it?"

"Well she is sick—ill, I mean."

"*She says*! How do you like it now you are here?"

"I like it all right, but the chilblains on my hands hurt."

Then she said I would have lots of time to find out if I did like it as she was leaving the next day to stay with friends at Thaxted. "Miss Born has all of Charlotte M. Yonge's novels lined up for you to read in the evenings."

"Oh Lord, she hasn't!"

"Just you wait," said Camilla.

The maid came in to light up and soon it would be time to go upstairs and change for dinner. I thought this woman one of the most fascinating I had ever seen. She had a long thin face, dead white, or powdered dead white. Her hair was black and lively under her cap, her eyes so small that the first time I saw her I thought she was blind. But wide open, they were the most astonishing blue, cornflower blue, no, more like sparks of blue fire. Then she would drop her eyelids and her face would go dead and lifeless again. I never tired of watching this transformation.

After dinner there I was, reading aloud *The Dove in the Eagle's Nest*. Camilla didn't listen, nor did Miss Rode, our headmistress, who was a middle-aged very imposing woman with quantities of black-grey hair arranged like a coronet. She dressed in various shades of brown, purple, puce or mustard and her face was serene and kind.

Miss Born however never took her eyes off me. Miss Born was old, she wore black, she never taught. She represented breeding and culture and was a great asset to the school. "Drop your voice," she would say, "drop it. An octave at least"; or "That will do, don't go on, I really cannot bear any more tonight."

We sat around the fire till the clock struck nine. "Goodnight Miss Rode." "Goodnight, dear child" said Miss Rode, who was wearing her purple, always a good sign. "Goodnight Miss Born." Miss Born inclined her head very slightly and as I went out remarked, "Why did you insist on that girl playing Autolycus? Tony Lumpkin in person."

"Not in person, surely," said Miss Rode mildly.

"In manner then, in manner," said Miss Born.

Camilla shut the door and I heard no more.

The staircase was slippery and smelt of floor polish. All the way up to the bedroom floor I thought about Miss Born's black clothes, her small active body. A mouse with a parrot's head. I hadn't even wanted to be in the old *Winter's Tale* and I told them so. However, I said nothing of all this to Camilla for I had been five months in England and was slowly learning to be cautious. Besides the bedrooms were unheated and I had already begun to shiver and shake.

"Don't you think it's frightfully cold, Camilla?"

"No, not particularly. Hop into bed and you'll soon get warm." She went off to her own room four doors away.

I knew of course that I would not sleep or get warm for on top of everything else an icy wind was blowing through the window, which for some mysterious reason must be left open six inches at the top.

Do not shut your window. This window must not be closed.

I was still awake and shivering, clutching my ankles with my hands, when the maid, who was called Jarvis, knocked. "I've brought you up a hot water bottle, miss."

"Oh thank you. How awfully kind of you."

"It is my own hot water bottle," she said. She asked why I didn't shut my window.

"Well, I thought we weren't supposed to."

She pushed the sash up without answering. I stretched my legs out and put the bottle where my back hurt and thanked her again. I hoped she'd go away but she lingered.

"I wanted to tell you, miss, that I enjoyed the school play this term very much. You were good in that boy's part."

"Autolycus."

"Well, I don't remember the name but you quite cheered me up."

"I'm very glad," I said. "Goodnight Jarvis, don't catch cold in this icy little room."

"I had a great success once in an amateur theatrical performance," she went on dreamily. "I played the part of a blind girl."

"You played a blind girl? How strange, because when I saw you first I thought. . . ." I stopped. "I thought you might be able to act because you don't look at all wooden."

"The flowers I had sent me," she said. "Roses and that. Of course, it was long ago, when I was a girl, but I still remember my part, every word of it."

"How very nice" was all I could think of to say. She snapped the light out and shut the door, rather loudly.

She played a blind girl. I thought she was blind. But this sort of thing had happened

to me before. I'd stopped trying to make
sense of clues that led nowhere.

When, next day after breakfast, Camilla
left I got through the morning thinking no
bicycle ride anyhow. Patey isn't here.

Miss Patey had been trying to teach me to
bicycle. She always skimmed gracefully
ahead as though she had nothing to do with
me and I followed her, wobbling dangerously
from side to side. Once when I'd fallen into a
ditch on the way to Newnham, she turned
back and asked in a detached way if I'd
hurt myself. "Oh no, Miss Patey, not at all."
I climbed out of the ditch and picked up the
bicycle. "I see your stocking is torn and that
is quite a bruise on your knee." She did not
speak again until we got to the Trumpington
Road. "You had better get down and wheel
your bicycle here." "Yes, Miss Patey."

Limping along the Trumpington Road . . .
past Mrs. G.'s house, a distant relative of my
father's. I was allowed to have tea with her
every Saturday afternoon. . . . She was called
Jeanette and was a very lovely, stately old
lady with thick white hair, huge black eyes
and a classic profile. She didn't wear spec-
tacles except for reading and her hands were
slender and transparent looking. She talked
about Cambridge when she was young and
the famous men she'd known. "Poor Darwin.
He threaded the labyrinths of creation and
lost his Creator." Or "Of course Fitzgerald's

translation from the Persian was not really accurate . . ."; and the Song of Solomon was an allegory of Christ and His Church.

Another day she told me that she had nearly eloped (tired of her absent-minded old husband, I suppose). She was packed and ready to leave but when she was pinning on her hat she saw in the looking-glass the devil grinning over her shoulder. She was so frightened that she changed her mind.

"And what did the devil look like?" I asked, very curious. But she never told me that.

Like so many beautiful old ladies then she had a devoted maid whom I was rather afraid of, she looked at me so sternly, so unsmilingly when she opened the door. Now I come to think of it, Jarvis didn't smile either.

None of the girls could believe that I'd never owned a bicycle before or that there were very few in the island. "How do you get about then, if there are no trains, buses, cars or bicycles?" they would say. "Horses, mules, carriages, buggies, traps." Winks, smiles. "Is it 'honey don't try so hard' or 'honey don't cry so hard'?" "How should I know?" "Well, it's a coon song, you ought to know." But when I discovered that though they never believed the truth, they swallowed the most fantastic lies, I amused myself a good deal.

That first afternoon when I had walked along the gravel path which circled the

muddy green hockey field, I crossed a flower
bed and looked into one of the dim classrooms. It was a grey-yellow day. Not so bad
as the white glaring days or the icy wind days.
Still, bad enough. The sky was the colour of
no hope, but they don't notice it, they are
used to it, they expect me to grow used to it.

It was while I was staring at the empty
ghostly-looking desks that I felt a lump in my
throat. Tears—my heart a heavy jagged
weight. Of course premonitions, presenti-
ments had brushed me before, cold and
clammy as a bat's wing, but nothing like
this. Despair, grey-yellow like their sky. I
stayed by the window in the cold thinking
"What is going to become of me? Why am
I here at all?"

One hot silent July afternoon I was told that
I was to go to England with my Aunt Clare,
who had been staying with us for the last six
months. I was to go to a school called The
Perse in Cambridge.

"It is very good of her to take charge of
you." I noticed that my father was looking at
me in a critical, disapproving way. "I am
sure," he said, "that it will do you a great deal
of good."

"I sincerely hope so," said Aunt Clare dubi-
ously.

This interview chilled me and I was silent
all that evening. (So, I noticed, was my

mother.) I went up to my bedroom early and took out the exercise book that I called "Secret Poems."

> *I am going to England*
> *What shall I find there?*
>
> *"No matter what*
> *Not what I sought" said Byron.*
>
> *Not what I sought,*
> *Not what I seek.*

I wrote no more poems for a very long time.

Unfortunately it was a grey lowering August in London, not cold but never bright or fresh. My Aunt Clare, a tireless walker, dragged me round to see all the sights and after a week I went to sleep in the most unlikely places; St. Paul's, Westminster Abbey, Madame Tussaud's, the Wallace Collection, the zoo, even a shop or two. She was a swift but absent-minded walker and I could easily lag behind and find a chair or bench to droop on.

"She can't help it," I heard her explain once. "It's the change of climate, but it can really be very annoying."

Mistake after mistake.

But I knew the exact day when I lost belief in myself and cold caution took control. It was when she bought me the ugly dress instead of the pretty wine-coloured one.

"It's a perfect fit," said the saleswoman, "and the young lady is so pale, she needs colour."

My aunt looked at the price ticket. "No, not at all suitable," she said and chose a drab dress which I disliked. I didn't argue for the big shop and the saleswoman whom I thought very beautiful bewildered me. But I was heartbroken. I'd have to appear before a lot of strange girls in this hideous garment. "They're bound to dislike me."

Outside in the hostile street we got into the hateful bus (always squashed up against perfect strangers—millions of perfect strangers in this horrible place). The bus wheels said "And *when* we say we've *always* won, and *when* they ask us *how* it's done." (You wouldn't dare say how you do it, not straight out you wouldn't, it's too damned mean the way you do it.)

At Cambridge I refused to say anything except "Oh yes, that's very nice indeed. This bridge, that building. King's College Chapel. Oh yes. Very nice."

"Is that all you can say about King's College Chapel?" said Miss Born disdainfully.

Privately I thought that a Protestant service was all wrong in King's College Chapel, that it missed the smell of incense, splendid vestments, Latin prayers. "You've forgotten that you stole it from the Catholics but it hasn't forgotten," I thought. Fortunately I didn't say this.

"They sang very nicely indeed."

Well, I walked up and down the hockey field till I'd stopped crying then went back to the small dining-room where there was always a blazing fire, I will say. But I could not eat anything and Miss Rode sent me to bed.

"I hear," she said, "that you feel the cold, so you'll find extra blankets and Jarvis will bring you up a hot water bottle and hot milk."

Lying in bed, warm and comfortable, I tried to argue my fears away. After all, it's only for another eighteen months at the worst and though I don't particularly want to go back, there it is, solid and safe, the street, the sandbox tree, the stone steps, the long gallery with the round table at the top. But I was astonished to discover how patchy, vague and uncertain my memory had become. I had forgotten so much so soon.

I remembered the stars, but not the moon. It was a different moon, but different in what way? I didn't know. I remembered the shadows of trees more clearly than the trees, the sound of rain but not the sound of my mother's voice. Not really. I remembered the smell of dust and heat, the coolness of ferns but not the scent of any of the flowers. As for the mountains, the hills and the sea, they were not only thousands of miles away, they were years away.

About three days before the holidays ended, Miss Rode handed me a letter from Switzerland. "But I don't know anyone in Switzerland."

"Open it and find out," she said.

I put the letter under my pillow for a time, thinking it would be something to look forward to the next morning, but I was too curious to wait. I opened it—it was signed Myrtle. I was disappointed. What on earth had Myrtle, a girl I hardly knew, to write to me about? This was the letter which was to change my life.

Dear West Indies,

I have been thinking about you a lot since I came to Switzerland, perhaps because my mother is getting divorced. I see now what a silly lot of fools we were about everything that matters and I don't think you are. It was all those words in *The Winter's Tale* that Miss Born wanted to blue pencil, you rolled them out as though you knew what they meant. My mother said you made the other girls look like waxworks and when you dropped your cap you picked it up so naturally, like a born actress. She says that you ought to go on the stage and why don't you? I like Switzerland all right. There are a lot of English here and my mother says what a pity! She can be very sarcastic. Let me hear from you soon. I felt I simply had to write this.

Yours ever,
Myrtle

I read this letter over and over again, then rolled about from side to side making up an answer. "Dear Myrtle, Thanks for letter. I did not know what the words meant. I just liked the sound of them. I thought your mother very pretty, but yes, a bit sarky."

Then I stopped writing the imaginary letter to Myrtle for suddenly, like an illumination, I knew exactly what I wanted to do. Next day I wrote to my father. I told him that I longed to be an actress and that I wanted to go to the Academy of Dramatic Art in Gower Street.

"I am *quite* sure. Please think very seriously about it. I don't mind this place and some of the mistresses are quite all right but it's really a waste of money my being here. . . ."

When the answer arrived it was yes and I was happier than I'd ever been in my life. Nothing could touch me, not praise, nor blame. Nor incredulous smiles. A new term had started but Myrtle hadn't come back and Camilla was still away in Thaxted.

"There is an entrance examination," they'd say. "You won't pass it."

"Yes I will," but really I was extremely nervous about this examination and surprised when I did pass. The judges had seemed so very bored. The place was not Royal then and was known colloquially as "Tree's School." It wasn't so choosy then perhaps.

My aunt installed me in an Upper Bedford Place boarding-house and left me to it; she strongly disapproved of the whole business. However she soon came back to London and took a small flat near Baker Street to see for herself how I was getting on.

"When you're stabbed in the back you fall like this, and when you're stabbed in front you fall like this, but if you stab yourself you fall differently. Like this."

"Is that all you've learnt?"

"No." I told her about fencing classes, ballet, elocution, gesture. And so on. "No plays?" she wanted to know. "Yes of course. I was Celia in *As You Like It* and we did Paolo and Francesca once." And I was Francesca in the little dark sitting-room.

" *Now I am free and gay,*
Light as a dancer when the strings begin
All ties that held me I cast off. . . .' "

"You'll find that very expensive," my aunt said.

I spent the vacation with relatives in Yorkshire and one morning early my uncle woke me with a cablegram of the news of my father's sudden death. I was quite calm and he seemed surprised, but the truth was that I hadn't taken it in, I didn't believe him.

Harrogate was full of music that late summer. Concertinas, harpists, barrel organs, singers. One afternoon in an unfamiliar street, listening to a man singing "It may be for years and it may be for ever", I burst into tears and once started I couldn't stop.

Soon I was packed off to responsible Aunt Clare in Wales. "You cry without reticence," she told me the day after I arrived. "And you watch me without reticence," I thought.

There was a calm slow-moving river called the Afon that flowed at the bottom of my aunt's garden. Walking up and down looking at the water she said that she could understand my grief. My father's death meant that it was impossible to keep me in London at a theatrical school. "Quite out of the question." She had heard from my mother who wished me to return home at once. I said that I didn't want to go, "not yet." "But you'll have to." "I won't. . . ."

Aunt Clare changed the subject. "What a lovely day. Straight from the lap of the gods" (she talked like that). As her voice went on I was repeating to myself "Straight from the lap of the gods".

At last we went up to London to do some

shopping for hot weather clothes and one
afternoon when she was visiting friends I
went to Blackmore's agency in the Strand
and after some palaver was engaged as one
of the chorus of a touring musical comedy.
I was astonished when Aunt Clare told me
that I'd behaved deceitfully, outrageously. A
heated argument followed.

She said that my contract had no legal
value at my age and threatened to stop me.
I said that if she stopped me I'd marry a
young man at the Academy whom I knew she
detested. He'd been to tea at the Marylebone
flat. "He may be a horrid boy but he's got a
lot of money." "How do you know that?" said
my aunt in a different voice, a sharp voice.

"He showed me the letter from his trustees.
He's twenty-one. Besides at the Academy
everyone knows who has money and who
hasn't. That's one thing they do know."

"If this young man is well-off you ought to
think very carefully before you answer him."

"I have answered him. I said no. But if you
interfere with my contract I'll marry him and
be miserable. And it will be your fault."

This went on for a long time. Then Aunt
Clare said that it was unfair to expect her to
deal with me, that she'd write to my mother.
"Perhaps we'll be rehearsing before she an-
swers," I said hopefully. But when my mother's letter arrived it was very vague. She
didn't approve, neither did she altogether dis-

approve. It seemed as if what with her grief for my father and her worry about money she was relieved that I'd be earning my own living in England. "Not much of a living," said my aunt.

"Some people manage. Why shouldn't I?"

The company was playing a musical comedy called *Our Miss Gibbs*. We rehearsed at the National Sporting Club somewhere in the Leicester Square/Covent Garden area. A large room with a stage up one end. Sometimes boxers would pass through looking rather shy on their way to other rooms, I supposed. It was foggy. First a black fog then a yellow one. I didn't feel well but I never missed a rehearsal. Once my aunt came with me and the girls approved of her so enthusiastically that I saw her in a new light. "Is that your auntie? Oh, isn't she nice."

She was a nice woman, I see that now. It was kind of her to take charge of me to please her favourite brother. But she wasn't exactly demonstrative. Even pecks on the cheek were very rare. And I craved for affection and reassurance. By far my nicest Cambridge memory was of the day an undergraduate on a bicycle knocked me flat as I was crossing the road. I wasn't hurt but he picked me up so carefully and apologized so profusely that I thought about him for a long time.

Talking to the other girls I realized that several of them dreaded the tour up North in the winter. We were going to Oldham, Bury, Leeds, Halifax, Huddersfield and so on. As for the boys, one of them showed me a sketch he'd done of a street in a northern town. He'd called it "Why we drink". But none of this prevented me from being excited and happy.

The man who engaged me at the agent's was at one rehearsal. He came up to me and said in a low voice: "Don't tell the other girls that you were at Tree's School. They mightn't like it." I hadn't any idea what he meant. But "No, I won't tell anybody," I promised.

Before the Deluge

When I first met Daisie she was playing
Lily Elsie's part in the English stage version
of the *Count of Luxembourg* (Lily was either
ill or had gone on holiday). She was a very
beautiful girl, perhaps the most beautiful girl
I have ever seen. I think sometimes that while
there are many more pretty and attractive
girls now, there are fewer raving beauties.

There was another beauty in the chorus of
the only pantomime I ever played in at the
Lyceum Theatre. Her name was Kyrle and I
was amused by the reactions of the Lyons
waitresses to her. Instead of the sharp, ap-
praising, flouncy glance that they'd give an
ordinarily pretty girl, an amazed, humble expression would come into their faces, the way
you'd look at Princess Graciosa or Sleeping
Beauty just awakened, if you met her out for
a walk.

Daisie was taller and more impressive than
Kyrle. She had dark red hair, only shoulder

length, but very thick and naturally wavy, huge blue eyes and long golden eyelashes which she never made up except for a little vaseline on the tips and on her eyelids. Sometimes she would add a touch of rouge if she thought she looked pale. She had classic features—not aquiline but Greek—a large, sweet mouth and white even teeth. She was rather tall for a musical comedy actress but slim and with a very good figure. I was quite surprised when I gradually learned how spiteful she was, though spiteful, I always felt, in an innocent way.

She gossiped in an ascending scale, exactly as the chorus gossiped. She would start comparatively mildly: "She's a tart of course", and end accusing the girl of every known and unknown vice. She seemed to get particularly annoyed if one of her friends married, especially if the man was rich or well-known. "She's not the sort of woman who ought to get married at all, considering the life she's led, and as for him, well everybody knows he's rotten with it. What a pair! God help their children—if they have any," she'd end piously. All this didn't prevent her from kissing the friend, when she next met her, and saying quite sincerely, often with tears in her eyes, "Darling, I hope you'll be so very happy."

She was really a very generous girl and could be impulsively kind. She was certainly kind to me in a rather patronizing way. Although I was so thin I used to wear long, tight whalebone stays. One expensive pair I had made my waist very small and the large satin bow in front supplied the necessary curves, I hoped. Daisie rocked with laughter at this garment and soon persuaded me to throw it away and wear a suspender belt. She didn't approve of my lace and ribboned underclothes either, which were out of fashion she told me. So I soon wore instead very close-fitting directoire knickers. Some of her suggestions were beyond me, I felt the cold too much, but it did sink in that the scantier my underclothes the better. Then she supervised my buying a suit and thus fitted out I was taken to see George Edwardes, the impresario of the day.

I was rather disappointed in "the guv'nor", as he was called, for I'd heard many lurid stories about him. He was a quiet man who gave me a cup of tea and some good advice—which of course I didn't take. However, he suggested that I should be in the chorus of his number one touring company visiting all the big towns—Manchester, Dublin, Edinburgh, Liverpool—and if all went well and there were good reports of me he promised that I should be in the next show at Daly's.

I was very pleased. It was decidedly a step up from working for the man who employed me then, who did everything on the cheap, even shipping us to Ireland on a cattle boat. We were all violently sick and as we trooped off at Cork I looked at the other girls and thought what a bedraggled lot we were. And no wonder.

Daisie and I got to know each other quite well and I was often at her flat near Marble Arch, which I chiefly remember for the artificial butterflies on the net at the windows and the curtains of her huge bed. Her battle-axe of a mother disliked me so I can't say that I always enjoyed my visits there, and I felt like a page, walking behind her into smart restaurants holding the flowers that had been given to her after the show. "I think I'd like a devilled bone," she would say.

She gave her age as twenty-four and couldn't have been much older, but she had been on the stage for years. She had started before she was ten as a pantomime fairy and gone on from there. She had worked in fit-ups (one night stands). Killing work, she said. She had been a music hall turn billed as the singing star and indeed she had a lovely soprano voice, fresh and true. She worked hard at her singing and still took lessons when I knew her. Her teacher, an Italian, had been a well-known opera singer and was very good, she said.

But it was no use. Her face, her voice, nothing seemed to get over the footlights. In Bond Street people would turn and stare at her admiringly. On stage she was just a very pretty girl among a lot of other pretty girls. Songs that would bring down the house when Lily Elsie sang them were only politely applauded. This puzzled Daisie and she thought about it. Of course she couldn't act. She was always Daisie, the Manchester policeman's daughter and not a Viennese opera star at all, or anything else she was trying to be.

When I first knew her she made fun of temperamental actresses and told me that after Lily Elsie's big scene, she'd faint when she came off. Two of the stage hands were stationed in the wings to catch her when she fell. She—Daisie—thought that this was a fake, all put on and the most utter nonsense.

But gradually she changed her mind. She no longer jeered at temperament. On the contrary, she told me that now she often felt giddy and ill and realized it was a very great strain. One night she too had almost fainted. She said this with a certain amount of pride, as if she'd achieved something.

Soon Daisie's near faints or faints were as much a matter of routine as ever Lily Elsie's had been and unfortunately they weren't confined to the theatre. More and more often if you argued with or even contradicted her she'd sigh, put her hand to her head and flop.

The butterflies vanished (I suppose someone had told her that they were sentimental). They were replaced by huge spiders. I hated

these things and looked nervously at them
whenever I went into her flat for I was never
quite sure that they weren't real. They were
too lifelike altogether, crawling up lamp-
shades or wallpaper.

One day she asked me to call and see her
about noon. She wanted to speak to me.
Something important. I knew that twelve
o'clock was very early for Daisie but got
there punctually. She opened the door dressed
for the street, greeted me shortly and coldly
and when we reached the sitting-room began
pacing up and down.

At last she said: "I hear you've been gossip-
ing and telling lies about me all over the
place. I think it's rather beastly, after all I've
done for you."

I said I never gossiped and certainly not
about her. Gossip didn't interest me. "And
who am I supposed to lie and gossip to?" I
spoke angrily because I was surprised and
rather hurt. Instead of answering Daisie
opened her eyes very wide, gave a little cry,
and crashed to the floor bringing down a
small table as she fell.

I was horrified. She seemed unconscious
and I didn't know what to do. I thought of
putting a cushion under her head, then remembered that it wasn't the right thing for
every faint. Brandy? But I didn't know where
it was kept.

I was still dithering when the door opened

and a man came into the room and stared
accusingly at me. He must have been waiting
to take her out to lunch. Then her mother
appeared from the kitchen; one look at her
and I knew I was in for a torrent of abuse. I
didn't feel that I could stand it and ran out of
the flat into the street. As I left I heard him
crooning: "My poor, darling little girl, whàt
have they done to you, my poor little sweet-
heart."

Very soon after this my life changed, everything changed and I never saw or heard of
Daisie again.

On Not Shooting
Sitting Birds

There is no control over memory. Quite soon you find yourself being vague about an event which seemed so important at the time that you thought you'd never forget it. Or unable to recall the face of someone whom you could have sworn was there for ever. On the other hand, trivial and meaningless memories may stay with you for life. I can still shut my eyes and see Victoria grinding coffee on the pantry steps, the glass bookcase and the books in it, my father's pipe-rack, the leaves of the sandbox tree, the wallpaper of the bedroom in some shabby hotel, the hairdresser in Antibes. It's in this way that I remember buying the pink milanese silk underclothes, the assistant who sold them to me and coming into the street holding the parcel.

I had started out in life trusting everyone and now I trusted no one. So I had few acquaintances and no close friends. It was perhaps in reaction against the inevitable loneliness of my life that I'd find myself doing bold, risky, even outrageous things without hesitation or surprise. I was usually disappointed in these adventures and they didn't have much effect on me, good or bad, but I never quite lost the hope of something better or different.

One day, I've forgotten now where, I met this young man who smiled at me and when we had talked a bit I agreed to have dinner with him in a couple of days' time. I went home excited, for I'd liked him very much, and began to plan what I should wear. I had a dress I quite liked, an evening cloak, shoes, stockings, but my underclothes weren't good enough for the occasion, I decided. Next day I went out and bought the milanese silk chemise and drawers.

So there we were seated at a table having dinner with a bedroom very obvious in the background. He was younger than I'd thought and stiffer and I didn't like him much after all. He kept eyeing me in such a wary, puzzled way. When we had finished our soup and the waiter had taken the plates away, he said: "But you're a lady, aren't you?" exactly as he might have said, "But you're really a snake or a crocodile, aren't you?"

"Oh no, not that you'd notice," I said, but this didn't work. We looked glumly at each

other across the gulf that had yawned between us.

Before I came to England I'd read many
English novels and I imagined I knew all
about the thoughts and tastes of various sorts
of English people. I quickly decided that to
distract or interest this man I must talk about
shooting.

I asked him if he knew the West Indies at
all. He said no, he didn't and I told him a long
story of having been lost in the Dominican
forest when I was a child. This wasn't true.
I'd often been in the woods but never alone.
"There are no parrots now," I said, "or very
few. There used to be. There's a Dominican
parrot in the zoo—have you ever seen it?—
a sulky bird, very old I think. However, there
are plenty of other birds and we do have
shooting parties. Perdrix are very good to eat,
but ramiers are rather bitter."

Then I began describing a fictitious West
Indian shooting party and all the time I talked
I was remembering the real thing. An old
shotgun leaning up in one corner of the room,
the round table in the middle where we
would sit to make cartridges, putting the shot
in, ramming it down with a wad of paper.
Gunpowder? There was that too, for I remember the smell. I suppose the boys were
trusted to be careful.

The genuine shooting party consisted of
my two brothers, who shared the shotgun,

some hangers-on and me at the end of the procession, for then I couldn't bear to be left out of anything. As soon as the shooting was about to start I would stroll away casually and when I was out of sight run as hard as I could, crouch down behind a bush and put my fingers in my ears. It wasn't that I was sorry for the birds, but I hated and feared the noise of the gun. When it was all over I'd quietly join the others. I must have done this unobtrusively or probably my brothers thought me too insignificant to worry about, for no one ever remarked on my odd behaviour or teased me about it.

On and on I went, almost believing what I was saying, when he interrupted me. "Do you mean to say that your brothers shot sitting birds?" His voice was cold and shocked.

I stared at him. How could I convince this man that I hadn't the faintest idea whether my brothers shot sitting birds or not? How could I explain now what really happened? If I did he'd think me a liar. Also a coward and there he'd be right, for I was afraid of many things, not only the sound of gunfire. But by this time I wasn't sure that I liked him at all so I was silent and felt my face growing as stiff and unsmiling as his.

It was a most uncomfortable dinner. We both avoided looking at the bedroom and when the last mouthful was swallowed he announced that he was going to take me home. The way he said this rather puzzled me. Then I told myself that probably he was curious to see where I lived. Neither of us spoke in the taxi except to say, "Well, goodnight." "Goodnight."

I felt regretful when it came to taking off my lovely pink chemise, but I could still think: Some other night perhaps, another sort of man.

I slept at once.

Kikimora

The bell rang. When Elsa opened the door a small, fair, plump young man advanced, bowed and said "Baron Mumtael".

"Oh yes, please come in," said Elsa. She was aware that her smile was shy, her manner lacking in poise, for she had found his quick downward and upward glance intimidating. She led the way and asked him to sit down.

"What a very elegant dinner suit you are wearing," said Baron Mumtael mockingly.

"Yes, isn't it? . . . oh, I don't think it is really," said Elsa distractedly. "I hate myself in suits," she went on, plunging deep into the scorn of his pale blue eyes.

"The large armchair is of course your husband's and the smaller one yours," said the baron quirking his mouth upwards. "What a typical interior! Where shall I sit?"

"Sit wherever you like," said Elsa. "The interior is all yours. Choose your favourite bit." But his cold glance quelled her and she added, twittering: "Will you . . . do have a drink."

Bottles of whisky, vermouth and soda water stood on a red lacquered tray. "I'll have vermouth," said Baron Mumtael firmly. "No soda, thank you. And you?"

"A whisky I think," Elsa said, annoyed that her hands had begun to shake with nervousness.

"How nice is ice on a hot afternoon. Are you . . . have you lived in America?"

"No. Oh, no." She gulped her whisky and soda quickly.

"Charming," said Baron Mumtael watching her maliciously, "charming. I'm so glad you're not an American. I think some American women are a menace, don't you? The spoilt female is invariably a menace."

"And what about the spoilt male?"

"Oh the spoilt male can be charming. No spoiling, no charm."

"That's what I always say," said Elsa eagerly. "No spoiling, no charm."

"No," said Baron Mumtael. "None. None at all. Will your husband be long do you think?"

"I think not. I think here he is."

After Stephen came in the tension lessened. Baron Mumtael stopped fidgeting and settled down to a serious discussion of the politics of his native land, his love of England and his joy at having at last become a naturalized Englishman.

Elsa went out of the room to put the finishing touches to the meal. It was good, she thought. He would have to appreciate it. And indeed, the first time he addressed her, after they sat down, he said: "What delicious food! I congratulate you."

"It all came from various shops in Soho," Elsa lied.

"Really delicious. And that picture fascinates me. What is it supposed to be?"

"Paradise."

A naked man was riding into a dark blue sea. There was a sky to match, palm trees, a whale in one corner, and a butterfly in the other. "Don't you like it?" she asked.

"Well," said Baron Mumtael, "I think it's colourful. It was painted by a woman, I feel sure."

"No, it was painted by a man," said Elsa. "He said he put in the whale and the butterfly because everything has its place in Paradise."

"Really," said Baron Mumtael, "I shouldn't have thought so. One can only hope not. Please tell me which shop in Soho supplied the guinea-fowl and really delicious sauté potatoes?"

"I've forgotten," said Elsa vaguely. "Somewhere around Wardour Street or Greek Street. I'm so bad at remembering where places are. Of course you have to fry the potatoes up with onions and then you get something like Pommes Lyonnaises."

But Baron Mumtael had already turned away and was continuing his conversation with Stephen about the next war. He gave it three months (and he wasn't far wrong).

The black cat, Kikimora, who had been sitting quietly in the corner of the room, sprang onto his lap. The Baron looked surprised, stroked the animal cautiously, then sprang up and said: "My God! She's scratched me, quite badly." And indeed there was blood on the finger he was holding up.

"I can't think what's come over him," Elsa said. "I've never known him do such a thing before. He's so staid as a rule. You naughty, bad cat." She snatched him up and flung him outside the door. "I'm so very sorry."

"Elsa spoils that cat," Stephen said.

"I think," said Baron Mumtael, "that something ought to be done about my finger. You can't be too careful about the scratches of a she-cat. If you'd be so kind as to let me have some disinfectant?"

"He's not a she-cat, he's a he-cat," said Elsa.

"Really," said Baron Mumtael. "Can you let me have some disinfectant? That is, if you have any," he added.

"I've got harpic and peroxide of hydrogen," said Elsa belligerently, repeated whiskies having given her courage. "Which will you have?"

"My *dear* Elsa. . . ." said Stephen.

She left them and locked herself in the bathroom. When she came back Baron Mumtael was still holding his finger up, talking politics.

"I haven't forgotten the cotton wool," she said.

At last the finger was disinfected and a spotless white handkerchief wrapped round it. "One can't be too careful with a she-cat," Baron Mumtael kept repeating. And Elsa, breathing deeply, would always answer, "He's not a she-cat, he's a he-cat."

"Goodbye," said Baron Mumtael as he left. "I shall never forget your charming evening's entertainment. Or your so very elegant dinner suit. It's been quite an experience. All so typical."

As soon as he was out of the door Elsa said: "What a horrible man!"

"I didn't think so," Stephen said. "I thought he was rather a nice chap, It's a relief to meet somebody who doesn't abuse the English."

"Abuse the English?" said Elsa. "He'd never abuse the English. It must be comforting to be able to take out naturalization papers when you find your spiritual home."

"You hardly shone," Stephen said.

"Of course I shone. He brought out all my sparkle. He was so nice, wasn't he?"

"I didn't notice that he wasn't nice," said Stephen.

"No. You wouldn't," Elsa muttered.

She went into the kitchen, caught up the cat and began to kiss it. "My darling cat. My darling black velvet cat with the sharp claws. My angel, my little gamecock. . . ."

Kikimora purred and even licked a tear off her face with his rough tongue. But when he struggled and she put him down he yawned elaborately and walked away.

Elsa went to the bedroom, took off the suit she had been wearing, and with the help of a pair of scissors began to tear it up. Stephen heard the rending noise and called out: "What on earth are you doing?"

"I'm destroying my feminine charm," Elsa said. "I thought I'd make a nice quick clean job of it."

Night Out 1925

It had been raining and the green and red reflections of the lights in the wet streets made Suzy think of Francis Carco's books. She was walking with a man called Gilbert, known to his acquaintances in Montparnasse as "stingy Bertie."

Gilbert, pointing out that the rain had stopped and that the fresh air would do them good, was taking her to a place which he said was great fun and a bit of a surprise.

They crossed the Seine and went on walking. Suzy was about to tell him that she was getting tired and must have a taxi when he stopped half-way up a quiet side street. They went down a few steps into a long narrow room lined with tall mirrors, and a woman dressed in black came forward.

"Bonsoir Madame," said Gilbert familiarly. "Comment allez vous? I've brought a friend to see you."

"Bonsoir Madame, bonsoir Monsieur," said the woman showing her teeth.

She doesn't know him from Adam, Suzy was thinking when she lost sight of her and they were surrounded by a crowd of girls in varying stages of nakedness. They arranged themselves in a pattern, the ones in front kneeling, the ones at the back standing. Their spiky eyelashes stuck out. They opened their mouths and fluttered their tongues at the visitors, not in derision as might be supposed, but in invitation.

I bet they are giving us the bird too, Suzy told herself.

"Choose one," said Gilbert. Suzy chose a small dark girl who she thought less alarming than the rest. Gilbert chose a much taller girl with red hair and a long chin. Rather like a mare.

The others melted away, presumably to wait for the next clients.

Suzy, Gilbert and their girls went to sit at one of several small empty tables at the other end of the room. A very old waiter shuffled up and asked what they'd have to drink.

"What stort of a man takes a job as waiter in a place like this?" said Gilbert in English but without lowering his voice. The girls asked for "deux cerises", Suzy and Gilbert for Pernod.

"He'll soon be dead," said Suzy when the

waiter had gone. "You needn't be so virtuous about him. He can hardly walk as it is."

"A good thing too," said Gilbert.

The music of a java reached them from some other room. The drinks arrived and the girls began to chat in an animated way but Gilbert answered briefly or not at all and Suzy was silent because she felt shy and couldn't think of anything appropriate to say. After this had gone on for some time the mare began to look sulky but the other girl seemed worried—a hostess who feared the party was going to be dull, trying to imagine a way to liven it up.

Eventually she turned to Suzy, lifted her skirt and kissed her knee.

"Tu es folle," said the mare.

"Mon amie n'aime pas ça," said Gilbert.

"Ah!" said the girl. She was wearing a very short white tunic, white socks and heelless black strap shoes. A brass medal hung round her neck. Her face was quite round. She looked rather stupid but sweet, Suzy thought, smiling and putting her hand on the small pump hand.

"Tut tut," said Gilbert. "What am I to make of this?"

"I suppose," said Suzy looking at him, "that if she got fed up here she could clear out. Could she?"

"Of course she could," said Gilbert. "I'll ask her."

"Mais certainement," said the girl. "Naturellement. Pourquoi pas?" When no one spoke, she added in a low voice, "seulement, seulement. . . ."

"Seulement what?" said Suzy. "Seulement what?"

"Oh do shut up Suzy," said Gilbert. "What's the matter with you? Why these idiotic questions?"

"Come upstairs," said the mare. "Come and see us do our 'cinéma'. You won't be disappointed."

She also had on a white tunic, white socks and black slippers, but the tunic was open to the waist in front.

"No," said Gilbert. "I think not." He went on speaking to Suzy: "This place has gone off dreadfully. It really used to be fun, it had an atmosphere. It's not the same thing at all now. Of course we are much too early. But still. . . ."

"We might give you a few ideas," said the mare. "You look as if you need them."

"Come along Suzy." He sounded vexed. "Finish your drink and we'll try somewhere else."

"I'm all for that," said Suzy, "because I really don't think I'm going down very well here. One of the girls at the other end of the room is going to come across and slap my face any minute."

"Which one?" said Gilbert turning to look. "Where?"

A girl with beautiful breasts and a very slim body was staring at her with an extremely angry expression.

"Very bad tempered," said Gilbert.

"She's getting quite het up," Suzy said.

"Yes I see," said Gilbert.

"She thinks I'm here to stare and jeer. You can't blame her."

The woman who had first met them came up to their table. "Are any of these girls annoying you?"

"Why no," said Suzy. "Absolutely not. We think them charming, don't we Gilbert?"

Gilbert didn't answer.

The woman glanced meaningly at the two girls and walked away.

"Venez donc," said the mare. "Come upstairs. For you it will be only three hundred francs. And the champagne."

"No," said Gilbert. "I regret but no. Not this evening," and in English, "That's quite enough of that. Let's depart."

The girls knew that the clients were dissatisfied and intended to leave.

The dark girl was silent. But the mare began a long rapid speech to which Gilbert listened with a wry smile.

"She wants us to stump up, of course," he said at last. "I suppose she thinks it a good idea to harp on the difficulties of her profession. Same old miseries. No splendours. Not any more. Sad, isn't it?" He laughed.

The dark girl jumped up and hit the table with her fist so hard that her glass fell over.

"Et qu'est-ce que tu yeux que ça leur fasse?" she said loudly. "Qu'est-ce que tu veux ça leur fasse?"

"Drama!" said Gilbert. "What do you think it matters to them, she said."

"Yes. Gilbert, we can't walk out and not give these girls a sou."

"They've had their drinks," said Gilbert.

"Two cherries in brandy. Not much. Let me give them something, will you?"

"Well," said Gilbert, "if I do, will you promise to come on somewhere else? Somewhere where they'll put a bit more pep into it."

"Yes," said Suzy, "if you want me to."

"All right. Here you are then." He handed her his wallet. "Give them each — —" He marked 10 on the table with his cigarette. "That's quite enough." He turned away to look at the angry girl.

Suzy opened his wallet and took out two notes. She folded them carefully and gave one to each girl. Each smiled and slipped the note into the top of her sock.

"You permit me?" said the dark one. She took off the medal and, giving it to Suzy, kissed her warmly. "I will be happy to see any friend of yours who visits Paris."

Dédé was printed on one side of the medal; on the other the address.

"Alors," said the mare briskly. "Merci bien m'sieur et dame. Au 'voir. A la prochaine."

"I wish they'd go away," Suzy said.

"Allez-vous-en," said Gilbert.

No one took any notice of them as they walked down the long room.

"Bonsoir Madame. Bonsoir Monsieur," said the woman at the door.

They were outside.

"That was rather a fiasco," Gilbert said. "Sorry. It won't be difficult to find a more amusing place. I'll get a taxi."

"Yes," said Suzy. "But perhaps I ought to tell you that I gave those girls a fiver each."

"You did what?" Gilbert said. He opened his wallet and was silent. His silence lasted so long that Suzy couldn't bear it any longer. She said excitedly: "Why shouldn't they have some money? Why shouldn't they have some money?"

"If you feel like that about it," said Gilbert, "why don't you try giving away your own instead of making free with someone else's?"

"Because I haven't got any," said Suzy. "That's easy."

"Of course," Gilbert said. "Other people are always expected to pay for your oh-so-beauti-

ful ideas. And all such bloody hypocrisy. You
don't care at all really. When you'd given
those girls my money you were only too
anxious to see the last of them, weren't you?"

"Oh no, it wasn't that," Suzy said. "I
thought we'd better go before there was any
chance of your finding out."

"What did you imagine I'd do? Make a
row? Try to get the money back?"

"I didn't know what you'd do," Suzy said.
"So it seemed best to get away quickly."

"Well thanks a lot." He walked on, to Suzy's
relief, still talking in a level voice.

"And it shows how little you know about
these things. If those girls had done all their
stunts, all their stunts, a hundred francs
would have been a royal tip. A royal tip.
You've given them ten pounds for nothing at
all. I'll be a laughing stock. That bit at the
end was a fake. It was the 'cinéma' for the
clients who can't be persuaded upstairs. And
you fell for it. I'll be a laughing stock," he
repeated.

"No, I don't think it was a fake," Suzy said.

But she remembered how confidingly he
had handed her his wallet and began to feel
guilty.

"Ten quid isn't so very much. And you had
a wad of fivers in that wallet. Was what I did
so awful? Just think how you'll be received
when you go back. The tall handsome En-

glishman who gives ten quid for nothing at all. You'll be a legend not a laughing stock."

They'd reached the end of the street.

"A bus that will take you back to Montparnasse stops near here," said Gilbert stiffly.

They waited. A woman's scarlet hat was lying in the gutter.

"Poor old hat," said Suzy. "Poor old hat. Someone ought to write a poem about that hat." She was still holding Dédé's medal.

"Just a word to the wise before we part," Gilbert said. "Don't hang onto that medal. I know you, you'll leave it on your night table and whoever brings up your breakfast will see it. Better not."

"They won't care either," said Suzy.

"That's what you think. Better not. Believe you me."

Suzy began to giggle. She arranged the medal carefully under the red hat and holding up her hand said solemnly, "Rest in Peace in the name of Allah the Compassionate, the Merciful."

"Here comes your bus," said Gilbert. "It stops quite near the Dôme and I suppose that you can find your way from there."

"Yes I'll be all right. Au 'voir Gilbert. A la prochaine."

"There's not going to be a next time," said Gilbert as he walked away.

Suzy got into the bus relieved that it was half empty. She sat down and listened to the voices in her head as she thought about the evening.

"Same old miseries. No more splendour. Not now. Et qu'est-ce que tu veux que ça leur fasse?"

The Chevalier
of the Place Blanche

*This story is a much-adapted translation
of one written by Edouard de Nève*

He was intimately acquainted with the police of three countries, and he sat alone in a small restaurant not far from the Boulevard Montparnasse sipping an apéritif moodily, for he disliked Montparnasse and detested solitude. He had left his native Montmartre to dine with a lady and had arrived twenty minutes late. She was not of those usually kept waiting and she had already departed.

"Sacré Floriane", muttered the Chevalier. He looked at a Swedish couple at the next table, at the bald American by the door, and at the hairy Anglo-Saxon novelist in the corner, and thought that they were a strange-looking lot, and exceedingly depressing. (Quelles gueules qu'ils ont, was how he put it.) The place was full, but he was certainly the only French client. Then he felt a draught:

115

someone had come in and left the door open.
He turned to scowl, and, as he did so, the
girl who had entered walked past him and
sat down in the chair opposite. She took possession of his table, as it were, without looking at him and with only a slight gesture of
apology. Evidently another foreigner. But the
presence of a youthful female was soothing,
and his ill humour vanished. She was a tall,
blonde girl, not beautiful, not pretty, not chic;
nevertheless, there was something. The Chevalier, who was used to labelling women accu-
rately, decided that she was of the species
femme du monde. Then he began to feel sure
that she was an artist, a painter, one of those
young people who come to Paris with the
express purpose of making the fortunes of all
the hotel and restaurant proprietors of the
quartier Montparnasse.

The girl spoke to the waiter. Her accent,
though slight, was unmistakable—English or
American. English, he decided, after carefully
observing her hat. At this point an old man,
carrying a concertina, came into the restaurant and asked permission to play. The pro-
prietor nodded from behind the counter, and
he began a waltz which the Chevalier vaguely
remembered having heard when a small boy.
He remarked aloud: "Tiens! That makes me
feel young again."

"It gives me the cafard," said the girl, answering him in French.

"Madame," said the Chevalier seriously, "one must kill a cafard at once, cruelly and without scruple." The girl laughed, but her eyes were so unhappy that he looked away from her, fearing that she was about to cry.

He said: "After all, it is always possible to kill a cafard. For that champagne is best. That costs money naturally, but there are other ways." She did not answer, and he went on: "Do you know Montmartre well?"

"No," she said. "Hardly at all."

"A pity. I live there. Shall I tell you about it?" He spoke in English.

She said hastily, "No, I understand you perfectly. Where did you learn your English? It doesn't matter, don't tell me. When you speak to me, will you speak French? I like your voice in French so much."

"Is that so?" he asked politely. "As you wish."

It was about an hour later that she said, "Will you take me to Montmartre tonight?"

"But certainly." He looked steadily at her with bright hard eyes. "Where?"

"I don't mind. Anywhere."

"Bon. We'll go about half past ten to look at Montmartre, and if you are still sad when we come back you are a neurasthénic. Hereditary, hopeless."

"All right," she said. "But there's one condition. I pay my share."

The Chevalier thought this reasonable, acceptable, and in no way contrary to his dignity as a male. He had the habit of pleasing women, but not of spending much money on them. Indeed he had organized his life quite otherwise.

They shook hands solemnly. "Come along," he said, "let's go and kill the cafard."

They took the métro. "Place J. B. Clément" she read as they emerged by the light of a street-lamp. "It sounds like a Deputy."

The Chevalier, who had seemed preoccupied, told her that J. B. Clément had been, on the contrary, a poet.

"He composed the most beautiful song in the world, the Temps des Cerises."

"I don't know it," she said.

"But you must know it." He stopped to gesticulate eagerly. "It begins like this: 'Lorsque reviendra le temps des cerises'." He sang the line in a voice that was suddenly grave and profound.

She said that she remembered vaguely that it was not a lively song.

"Comment, not lively?" He sounded scandalized. "It is beautiful, and that is enough. It finishes: 'Profitez en bien des temps des cerises. . . .' There's a good advice for you." He began to laugh and walked on.

She glanced sideways at him. Childlike, that's what he was. What could he possibly do to earn his living, she wondered, and ended by asking him.

"I work in an office."

"You work in an office?" she said, astonished.

"Yes. I cheat Americans before they have time to cheat me."

"You do it first," she said. "A good motto."

He repeated, delighted, "That's it! I do it first. Look at the grey house opposite. I live there. One evening, will you come to see me and look down on the lights of Paris?"

They were at the end of the old Rue Vincent.

"Oh, but it's beautiful here," she said.

"You must see it from my window," insisted the Chevalier.

He tried to see the expression of her eyes, for he felt that there was only one logical end to all this, but she neither answered nor looked at him, and her height and what seemed to him the extraordinary austerity of her clothes were rather alarming. He added hastily that that would be for another evening.

They went to a nightclub but after an hour she told him that she wished to go home. "The cafard is dead for the moment."

In the taxi he asked her name. "Margaret Lucas. And you? I imagine that a letter addressed to the Chevalier of the Place Blanche won't find you" (for she had heard someone in the nightclub hail him by that name—how was she to know with what irony?).

"Ah, you wish to write to me?" he asked eagerly.

"Perhaps. Next time I have a cafard."

He told her ceremoniously: "Maurice Fernande, 139 Rue Vincent. Pour vous servir, Mees Margaret."

"No—Just Margaret."

He said: "We should drink *Auf Bruderschaft* as the Germans do."

"Some other evening."

"Haven't you got any relations here, Margaret? It must be lonely for a young girl by herself in Paris."

"I'm not a young girl," she answered indifferently, "and I've several friends here."

"Send me a pneu when you wish to see me."

The street was deserted; the last métro had gone, and as a taxi willing to climb to the Butte at that hour would be expensive, he decided to walk. As he walked he calculated his chances of escape from a very unfortunate situation. He should not have wasted an evening, evidently.

It was perfectly true that he worked in a Tourist Office. He had waited his opportunity there for three long months. At length the opportunity had come. A cheque for thirty thousand francs had disappeared to be converted, as he knew only too well, into a couple of Impressionist pictures fabricated by a friend of his, and several new suits of clothes.

Things had not gone according to plan. He had not resold the pictures nearly as profitably as he had hoped and he would have to give an account of the cheque much sooner than he had expected. Well, what did it matter, he thought? He could find the money. He could always find the money. There were many women in the world and for what purpose but to aid and comfort in just such an emergency?

There was the Baronne, a doubtfully authentic Baronne, but her money was authentic enough; there was Madame Yda, who had lately set up in business as a Grande Couturière. Both these ladies had some affection for him and had never hesitated to prove it in more ways than one. As for the Englishwoman . . . perhaps Fate had sent him the Englishwoman, and he looked anything but childlike as he thought it.

During the following week he got busy, calling several times at the hotel of his friend, the Baronne, always to be told that Madame was unable to receive him. He wrote and his letter was unanswered. She was obviously suspicious or resentful and he concluded, without wasting time on vain regrets, that there was nothing doing. And addressed himself to Madame Yda.

That lady observed him carefully with the

eyes of an intelligent monkey; she was thin,
elegant and wore pearls, which, if real, were
certainly worth having. He spoke lengthily
and fluently.

"Sorry mon vieux," she said when he had
finished. "Business is bad just now. Besides,
one never sees you except you want money.
That is not clever of you. Thirty thousand
francs is a sum."

"Then it's no?" he demanded.

"For the moment, impossible."

"Very well, we won't speak of it."

When she asked him, with a hesitation not
without pathos, if he would dine with her
that evening—sans rancune—"Impossible" he
said, smiling charmingly, and added with his
most insolent expression: "I've something better to do, ma vieille!"

He departed without giving her time to
answer and went home deep in thought. In
his pocket was a pneumatique from Margaret
which informed him that she would dine with
him that evening in Rue Vincent. They had
seen each other several times and the second
time they had met she had confided in him.
At least she had said that she was tired of
Paris and wished to go to Austria or Spain—
yes Spain; she had many things to forget, and
he had instantly diagnosed an unhappy love
affair. He had not encouraged her to give details for all unhappy love affairs are alike and
he had heard the history of so many. He

thought that women were all the same; they complicated things in the most idiotic fashion. He began to discuss with real interest the details of her tour in Spain.

He calculated rapidly. Yes, this must be her last night in Paris. He knew the importance of a mise-en-scène on these occasions and he bought crimson roses to place in a yellow vase, white roses for a black one. He bought things to eat which he supposed English girls to like. He bought two bottles of Extra Dry. He tied two pink silk handkerchiefs over the crude electric light and strewed cushions from his divan (of which he was very proud) on the floor. Finally he arrayed himself in the garment or garments which he called his "smoking" and sat down to wait. He made no definite plans—he seldom planned things in detail—but her conquest had now become a necessity.

She arrived rather late wearing a dress which, though she had bought it in a French shop, yet gave the impression of being completely English. She admired the roses and the view but did not appear to notice the smoking.

They stood at the window looking down on a glittering silhouette of Paris and he took her hand, kissed it and was instantly possessed with a real wish to kiss her mouth and an intense curiosity. It was with genuine desire that he tried to take her into his arms.

"Don't do that. I dislike it very much." Her voice was calm, she had not even moved, but his arms dropped to his sides and he stared at her as if she had flung icy water in his face.

Why then had she come? Was the little fool trying to provoke him? Then he remembered having heard that the English, before becoming animated, must be given something to drink, and without a word he brought her an apéritif. But he was a temperamental animal and all his élan had departed; he looked gloomy and resentful as they sat down at the carefully decorated little table. She would give him money all the same before she left—la garce.

Towards the end of the meal she said: "Tell me, Maurice, will you come and join me in Madrid?"

"I?" he said. "I come to Madrid! Ah, if I could—if I had the money. But voilà. Remember the office I told you about? I owe thirty thousand francs there and I must give them back tomorrow or I'm fichu, done for."

"Give them back then," she advised.

"You have good ideas," he said with a rather embarrassed laugh. "I to give them back trente mille balles? Why, I haven't the first sou of it!"

"I will give you the money," she said, lighting a cigarette and watching him thoughtfully.

"You will give me thirty thousand francs! Mon Dieu, but this is funny."

"On condition that you come with me to Madrid. We can send the money from there. Is it amusing, Madrid?"

He answered mechanically: "I think Madrid is ugly—Seville is beautiful."

She drew a deep breath and thought: "Seville."

"What do you find strange in all this? If you knew how unutterably bored I am, how much I disliked my life, you wouldn't find anything I did to get away from it strange. I think it's a very reasonable bargain indeed. I'll give you the money you need—I've got lots of money—you will try to amuse me and make me happier. I'm not asking you to make love to me, I've a horror of that sort of thing . . . A horror," she repeated.

He listened with a growing uneasiness as she went on picturing their life together in Spain. "I think you are a type, Maurice. You make me see things more vividly and I want to study you. I'm sick of trying to paint," she said. "I want to write a book about the modern Apache."

"The modern Apache!" echoed the Chevalier. And my smoking then, he thought indignantly, hasn't the woman noticed my smoking? Does she think that an Apache. . . .

"Well they do exist, don't they?"

He answered with a shrug. "Oh yes, they

existed. And plus ça change, plus c'est la
même chose."

"And they're brutal, reckless, all that?" She
quoted in a cold amused voice: "Du sang, de
la volupté, de la mort."

He did not answer her. He was utterly
taken aback.

"In any case, you interest me," she said.
Then, seemingly possessed by a devastating
wish to be frank, added: "As a type—not as
a man."

She considered him in a manner which
stung his masculine pride to the quick and
turned his uneasiness into definite revolt. He
did not know which revolted him more, the
idea of trailing about Seville at the orders of
this woman who was neither pretty nor chic,
or the idea that she believed him capable—
he, the conqueror of women—of playing such
a role.

"Non, merde alors! . . ." he thought. He
felt hot with rage and resentment and, forget-
ful of everything but his rage and his desire to
triumph over her, he made a superb gesture.

"Don't let's talk about it, Margaret. Tomorrow morning you will be on your way to
Spain and I will be here in my bed and that
is all. I to come away with you? I? But you
would be so unhappy with me as you have
never been in your life, my poor girl. Apaches!
Apaches. . . . And then? To write books is not
what an Apache needs of a woman, I tell you

that. You say you have a horror of this and a horror of that. I have a horror of a woman who talks and talks and never feels anything. It's all literature, what you say."

For the first time she dropped her eyes. "I've vexed you. I didn't mean to."

He stared at her sulkily, with dislike.

She stared back, then said, "I suppose I'd better go. I've enjoyed this evening. It's a pity that . . . oh well, it doesn't matter. Don't come with me on any account. I can find my own way to the métro." She put on her hat without looking in the glass, the unnatural creature.

He longed to do something violent to break down that air of cool friendliness, but the desire to live up to his smoking was too strong. He bowed stiffly and stood listening to the sound of her low heels descending the uncarpeted stairs. Nothing for it now but the midnight train to Brussels and a very thin time indeed.

The Insect World

Audrey began to read. Her book was called *Nothing So Blue*. It was set in the tropics. She started at the paragraph which described the habits of an insect called the jigger.

Almost any book was better than life, Audrey thought. Or rather, life as she was living it. Of course, life would soon change, open out, become quite different. You couldn't go on if you didn't hope that, could you? But for the time being there was no doubt that it was pleasant to get away from it. And books could take her away.

She could give herself up to the written word as naturally as a good dancer to music or a fine swimmer to water. The only difficulty was that after finishing the last sentence she was left with a feeling at once hollow and uncomfortably full. Exactly like indigestion. It was perhaps for this reason that she never forgot that books were one thing and that life was another.

When it came to life Audrey was practical. She accepted all she was told to accept. And there had been quite a lot of it. She had been in London for the last five years but for one short holiday. There had been the big blitz, then the uneasy lull, then the little blitz, now the fly·bombs. But she still accepted all she was told to accept, tried to remember all she was told to remember. The trouble was that she could not always forget all she was told to forget. She could not forget, for instance, that on her next birthday she would be twenty-nine years of age. Not a Girl any longer. Not really. The war had already gobbled up several years and who knew how long it would go on. Audrey dreaded growing old. She disliked and avoided old people and thought with horror of herself as old. She had never told anyone her real and especial reason for loathing the war. She had never spoken of it—even to her friend Monica.

Monica, who was an optimist five years younger than Audrey, was sure that the war would end soon.

"People always think that wars will end soon. But they don't," said Audrey. "Why, one lasted for a hundred years. What about that?"

Monica said: "But that was centuries ago and quite different. Nothing to do with Now."

But Audrey wasn't at all sure that it was so very different.

"It's as if I'm twins," she had said to Monica one day in an attempt to explain herself. "Do you ever feel like that?" But it seemed that Monica never did feel like that or if she did she didn't want to talk about it.

Yet there it was. Only one of the twins accepted. The other felt lost, betrayed, forsaken, a wanderer in a very dark wood. The other told her that all she accepted so meekly was quite mad, potty. And here even books let her down, for no book—at least no book that Audrey had ever read—even hinted at this essential wrongness or pottiness.

Only yesterday, for instance, she had come across it in *Nothing So Blue*. *Nothing So Blue* belonged to her, for she often bought books —most of them Penguins, but some from second-hand shops. She always wrote her name on the fly-leaf and tried to blot out any signs of previous ownership. But this book had been very difficult. It had taken her more than an hour to rub out the pencil marks that had been found all through it. They began harmlessly, "Read and enjoyed by Charles Edwin Roofe in this Year of our Salvation MCMXLII, which being interpreted is Thank You Very Much", continued "Blue? Rather pink, I think", and, throughout the whole of the book, the word "blue"—which of course often occurred—was underlined and in the

margin there would be a question mark, a
note of exclamation, or "Ha, ha." "Nauseat-
ing", he had written on the page which began
"I looked her over and decided she would
do". Then came the real love affair with the
beautiful English girl who smelt of daffodils
and Mr. Roofe had relapsed into "Ha, ha—
sez you!" But it was on page 166 that Audrey
had a shock. He had written "Women are an
unspeakable abomination" with such force
that the pencil had driven through the paper.
She had torn the page out and thrown it into
the fireplace. Fancy that! There was no fire,
of course, so she was able to pick it up,
smooth it out and stick it back.

"Why should I spoil my book?" she had
thought. All the same she felt terribly down
for some reason. And yet, she told herself, "I
bet if you met that man he would be awfully
ordinary, just like everybody else." It was
something about his small, neat, precise handwriting that made her think so. But it was
always the most ordinary things that suddenly turned round and showed you another
face, a terrifying face. That was the hidden
horror, the horror everybody pretended did
not exist, the horror that was responsible for
all the other horrors.

The book was not so cheering, either. It
was about damp, moist heat, birds that did
not sing, flowers that had no scent. Then there
was this horrible girl whom the hero simply

had to make love to, though he didn't really want to, and when the lovely, cool English girl heard about it she turned him down.

The natives were surly. They always seemed to be jeering behind your back. And they were stupid. They believed everything they were told, so that they could be easily worked up against somebody. Then they became cruel—so horribly cruel, you wouldn't believe. . . .

And the insects. Not only the rats, snakes and poisonous spiders, scorpions, centipedes, millions of termites in their earth-coloured nests from which branched out yards of elaborately built communication lines leading sometimes to a smaller nest, sometimes to an untouched part of the tree on which they were feeding, while sometimes they just petered out, empty. It was no use poking at a nest with a stick. It seemed vulnerable, but the insects would swarm, whitely horrible, to its defence, and would rebuild it in a night. The only thing was to smoke them out. Burn them alive-oh. And even then some would escape and at once start building somewhere else.

Finally, there were the minute crawling unseen things that got at you as you walked along harmlessly. Most horrible of all these was the Jigger.

Audrey stopped reading. She had a headache. Perhaps that was because she had not had anything to eat all day; unless you can count a cup of tea at eight in the morning as something to eat. But she did not often get a weekday off and when she did not a moment must be wasted. So from ten to two, regardless of sirens wailing, she went shopping in Oxford Street, and she skipped lunch. She bought stockings, a nightgown and a dress. It was buying the dress that had taken it out of her. The assistant had tried to sell her a print dress a size too big and, when she did not want it, had implied that it was unpatriotic to make so much fuss about what she wore. "But the colours are so glaring and it doesn't fit. It's much too short," Audrey said.

"You could easily let it down."

Audrey said: "But there's nothing to let down. I'd like to try on that dress over there."

"It's a very small size."

"Well, I'm thin enough," said Audrey defiantly. "How much thinner d'you want me to be?"

"But that's a dress for a girl," the assistant said.

And suddenly, what with the pain in her back and everything, Audrey had wanted to cry. She nearly said "I work just as hard as you," but she was too dignified.

"The grey one looks a pretty shape," she said. "Not so drear. Drear," she repeated, because that was a good word and if the

assistant knew anything she would place her
by it. But the woman, not at all impressed,
stared over her head.

"The dresses on that rail aren't your size.
You can try one on if you like but it wouldn't
be any use. You could easily let down the
print one," she repeated maddeningly.

Audrey had felt like a wet rag after her
defeat by the shop assistant, for she had
ended by buying the print dress. It would not
be enough to go and spruce up in the Ladies'
Room on the fifth floor—which would be
milling full of Old Things—so she had gone
home again, back to the flat she shared with
Monica. There had not been time to eat anything, but she had put on the new dress and
it looked even worse than it had looked in
the shop. From the neck to the waist it was
enormous, or shapeless. The skirt, on the other
hand, was very short and skimpy and two
buttons came off in her hand; she had to wait
and sew them on again.

It had all made her very tired. And she
would be late for tea at Roberta's. . . .

"I wish I lived here," she thought when she
came out of the Tube station. But she often
thought that when she went to a different
part of London. "It's nicer here," she'd think.
"I might be happier here."

Her friend Roberta's house was painted
green and had a small garden. Audrey felt
envious as she pressed the bell. And still more

envious when Roberta came to the door wearing a flowered house coat, led the way into a
pretty sitting-room and collapsed onto her
sofa in a film-star attitude. Audrey's immediate thought was "What right has a woman
got to be lolling about like that in wartime,
even if she is going to have a baby?" But
when she noticed Roberta's deep-circled eyes,
her huge, pathetic stomach, her spoilt hands,
her broken nails, and realized that her house
coat had been made out of a pair of old
curtains ("not half so pretty as she was.
Looks much older") she said the usual things,
warmly and sincerely.

But she hoped that, although it was nearly
six by the silver clock, Roberta would offer
her some tea and cake. Even a plain slice of
bread—she could have wolfed that down.

"Why are you so late?" Roberta asked. "I
suppose you've had tea," and hurried on before Audrey could open her mouth. "Have a
chocolate biscuit."

So Audrey ate a biscuit slowly. She felt she
did not know Roberta well enough to say
"I'm ravenous. I must have something to eat."
Besides that was the funny thing. The more
ravenous you grew, the more impossible it
became to say "I'm ravenous!"

"Is that a good book?" Roberta asked.

"I brought it to read on the Tube. It isn't
bad."

Roberta flicked through the pages of *Noth-*

ing So Blue without much interest. And she said "English people always mix up tropical places. My dear, I met a girl the other day who thought Moscow was the capital of India! Really, I think it's dangerous to be as ignorant as that, don't you?"

Roberta often talked about "English" people in that way. She had acquired the habit, Audrey thought, when she was out of England for two years before the war. She had lived for six months in New York. Then she had been to Miami, Trinidad, Bermuda—all those places—and no expense spared, or so she said. She had brought back all sorts of big ideas. Much too big. Gadgets for the kitchen. An extensive wardrobe. Expensive makeup. Having her hair and nails looked after every week at the hairdresser's. There was no end to it. Anyway, there was one good thing about the war. It had taken all that right off. Right off.

"Read what he says about jiggers," Audrey said.

"My dear," said Roberta, "he *is* piling it on."

"Do you mean that there aren't such things as jiggers?"

"Of course there are such things," Roberta said, "but they're only sand fleas. It's better not to go barefoot if you're frightened of them."

She explained about jiggers. They had

nasty ways—the man wasn't so far wrong.
She talked about tropical insects for some
time after that; she seemed to remember
them more vividly than anything else. Then
she read out bits of *Nothing So Blue,* laughing at it.

"If you must read all the time, you needn't
believe everything you read."

"I don't," said Audrey. "If you knew how
little I really believe you'd be surprised. Perhaps he doesn't see it the way you do. It all
depends on how people see things. If someone wanted to write a horrible book about
London, couldn't he write a horrible book?
I wish somebody would. I'd buy it."

"You dope!" said Roberta affectionately.

When the time came to go Audrey walked
back to the Tube station in a daze, and in a
daze sat in the train until a jerk of the brain
warned her that she had passed Leicester
Square and now had to change at King's
Cross. She felt very bad when she got out,
as if she could flop any minute. There were
so many people pushing, you got bewildered.

She tried to think about Monica, about the
end of the journey, above all about food—
warm, lovely food—but something had happened inside her head and she couldn't con-
centrate. She kept remembering the termites.
Termites running along one of the covered
ways that peter out and lead to nothing.
When she came to the escalator she hesitated,

afraid to get on it. The people clinging to the sides looked very like large insects. No, they didn't *look* like large insects: they were insects.

She got onto the escalator and stood staidly on the righthand side. No running up for her tonight. She pressed her arm against her side and felt the book. That started her thinking about jiggers again. Jiggers got in under your skin when you didn't know it and laid eggs inside you. Just walking along, as you might be walking along the street to a Tube station, you caught a jigger as easily as you bought a newspaper or turned on the radio. And there you were—infected—and not knowing a thing about it.

In front of her stood an elderly woman with dank hair and mean-looking clothes. It was funny how she hated women like that. It was funny how she hated most women anyway. Elderly women ought to stay at home. They oughtn't to walk about. Depressing people! Jutting out, that was what the woman was doing. Standing right in the middle, instead of in line. So that you could hardly blame the service girl, galloping up in a hurry, for giving her a good shove and saying under her breath "Oh get out of the way!" But she must have shoved too hard for the old thing tottered. She was going to fall. Audrey's heart jumped sickeningly into her mouth as she shut her eyes. She didn't want

to see what it would look like, didn't want
to hear the scream.

But no scream came and when Audrey
opened her eyes she saw that the old woman
had astonishingly saved herself. She had only
stumbled down a couple of steps and
clutched the rail again. She even managed to
laugh and say "Now I know where all the
beef goes to!" Her face, though, was very
white. So was Audrey's. Perhaps her heart
kept turning over. So did Audrey's.

Even when she got out of the Tube the
nightmare was not over. On the way home
she had to walk up a little street which she
hated and it was getting dark now. It was
one of those streets which are nearly always
empty. It had been badly blitzed and Audrey
was sure that it was haunted. Weeds and
wild-looking flowers were growing over the
skeleton houses, over the piles of rubble.
There were front doorsteps which looked as
though they were hanging by a thread, and
near one of them lived a black cat with green
eyes. She liked cats but not this one, not this
one. She was sure it wasn't a cat really.

Supposing the siren went? "If the siren
goes when I'm in this street it'll mean that it's
all U.P. with me." Supposing a man with a
strange blank face and no eyebrows—like
that one who got into the Ladies at the
cinema the other night and stood there grinning at them and nobody knew what to do so

everybody pretended he wasn't there. Perhaps he was *not* there, either—supposing a man like that were to come up softly behind her, touch her shoulder, speak to her, she wouldn't be able to struggle, she would just lie down and die of fright, so much she hated that street. And she had to walk slowly because if she ran she would give whatever it was its opportunity and it would run after her. However, even walking slowly, it came to an end at last. Just round the corner in a placid ordinary street where all the damage had been tidied up was the third floor flat which she shared with Monica, also a typist in a government office.

The radio was on full tilt. The smell of cabbage drifted down the stairs. Monica, for once, was getting the meal ready. They ate out on Mondays, Wednesdays and Fridays, in on Tuesdays, Thursdays, Saturdays and Sundays. Audrey usually did the housework and cooking and Monica took charge of the ration books, stood in long queues to shop and lugged the laundry back and forwards every week because the van didn't call any longer.

"Hullo," said Monica.

Audrey answered her feebly, "Hullo."

Monica, a dark, pretty girl, put the food on the table and remarked at once, "You're a bit green in the face. Have you been drinking mock gin?"

"Oh, don't be funny. I haven't had much to eat today—that's all."

After a few minutes Monica said impatiently, "Well why don't you eat then?"

"I think I've gone past it," said Audrey, fidgeting with the sausage and cabbage on her plate.

Monica began to read from the morning paper. She spoke loudly above the music on the radio.

"Have you seen this article about being a woman in Germany? It says they can't get any scent or eau-de-cologne or nail polish."

"Fancy that!" Audrey said. "Poor things!"

"It says the first thing Hitler stopped was nail polish. He began that way. I wonder why. He must have had a reason, mustn't he?"

"Why must he have had a reason?" said Audrey.

"Because," said Monica, "if they've got a girl thinking she isn't pretty, thinking she's shabby, they've got her where they want her, as a rule. And it might start with nail polish, see? And it says: 'All the old women and the middle-aged women look most terribly unhappy. They simply *slink* about it,' it says."

"You surprise me," Audrey said. "Different in the Isle of Dogs, isn't it?"

She was fed up now and she wanted to be rude to somebody. "Oh *do* shut up," she said. "I'm not interested. Why should I have to cope with German women as well as all the women over here? What a nightmare!"

Monica opened her mouth to answer sharply; then shut it again. She was an even-tempered girl. She piled the plates onto a tray, took it into the kitchen and began to wash up.

As soon as she had gone Audrey turned off the radio and the light. Blissful sleep, lovely sleep, she never got enough of it. . . . On Sunday mornings, long after Monica was up, she would lie unconscious. A heavy sleeper, you might call her, except that her breathing was noiseless and shallow and that she lay so still, without tossing or turning. And then *She (who?) sent the gentle sleep from Heaven that slid into my soul. That slid into my soul. Sleep, Nature's sweet, something-or-the-other. The sleep that knits up the ravelled.* . . .

It seemed that she had hardly shut her eyes when she was awake again. Monica was shaking her.

"What's the matter? Is it morning?" Audrey said. "What is it? What is it?"

"Oh, nothing at all," Monica said sarcastically. "You were only shrieking the place down."

"Was I?" Audrey said, interested. "What was I saying?"

"I don't know what you were saying and I don't care. But if you're trying to get us

turned out, that's the way to do it. You know
perfectly well that the woman downstairs is
doing all she can to get us out because she
says we are too noisy. You said something
about jiggers. What *are* jiggers anyway?"

"It's slang for people in the Tube," Audrey
answered glibly to her great surprise. "Didn't
you know that?"

"Oh is it? No, I never heard that."

"The name comes from a tropical insect,"
Audrey said, "that gets in under your skin
when you don't know it. It lays eggs and
hatches them out and you don't know it. And
there's another sort of tropical insect that
lives in enormous cities. They have railways,
Tubes, bridges, soldiers, wars, everything we
have. And they have big cities, and smaller
cities with roads going from one to another.
Most of them are what they call workers.
They never fly because they've lost their
wings and they never make love either.
They're just workers. Nobody quite knows
how this is done, but they think it's the food.
Other people say it's segregation. Don't you
believe me?" she said, her voice rising. "Do
you think I'm telling lies?"

"Of course I believe you," said Monica
soothingly, "but I don't see why you should
shout about it."

Audrey drew a deep breath. The corners
of her mouth quivered. Then she said "Look
I'm going to bed. I'm awfully tired. I'm go-

ing to take six aspirins and then go to bed. If the siren goes don't wake me up. Even if one of those things seems to be coming very close, don't wake me up. I don't want to be woken up whatever happens."

"Very well," Monica said. "All right, old girl."

Audrey rushed at her with clenched fists and began to shriek again. "Damn you, don't call me that. Damn your soul to everlasting hell *don't call me that....*"

Rapunzel, Rapunzel

During the three weeks I had been in the hospital I would often see a phantom village when I looked out of the window instead of the London plane trees. It was an Arab village or my idea of one, small white houses clustered together on a hill. This hallucination would appear and disappear and I'd watch for it, feeling lost when a day passed without my seeing it.

One morning I was told that I must get ready to leave as I was now well enough for a short stay in a convalescent home. I had to dress and get packed very quickly and what between my haste and unsteady legs I got into the car waiting outside the hospital without any idea of where it was going to take me.

We drove for about forty minutes, stopping twice to pick up other patients. We were still in London but what part of London? Norwood perhaps? Richmond? Beckenham?

The convalescent home, when we reached

it, was an imposing red brick building with
a fairly large garden. The other patients went
into a room on the ground floor and I walked
up the staircase by myself, clutching the
banisters. At the top a pretty but unsmiling
Indian nurse greeted me, showed me into a
ward, helped me unpack and saw me into
bed. There was a lot of talking and laughing
going on and a radio was playing; it was
confusing after the comparative quiet of the
hospital. I shut my eyes and when I opened
them a young good-looking doctor was standing near me. He asked a few questions and
finally where my home was.

"I live in Devon now."

"And have you been to any hunt balls
lately?"

This was so unexpected that it was a second or two before I managed to smile and say
that they must be great fun but that I'd never
been to a hunt ball and didn't know what
they were like. He lost interest and went over
to the next bed.

I couldn't sleep for a long time, the radio
and the conversation went on interminably
and I was relieved when, early next morning,
a nurse told me that I was to be moved into
another room.

The new ward was smaller and quieter.
There were about fourteen patients but I
was still too weary to notice anybody except
my immediate neighbour, an elderly woman

with piles of glossy magazines at the foot of her bed. She pored over them and played her radio all day. That night we had an argument, she said I ought to put my light out and not keep everybody awake because I wanted to read, I said that it wasn't yet ten o'clock and that her radio had annoyed me all day, but I soon gave in. Perhaps I was keeping the others awake.

Somebody was snoring; just as I thought the noise had stopped it would start up louder than ever and though I had asked for a sleeping pill, it seemed hours before it worked and when I did eventually sleep I had a long disturbing dream which I couldn't remember when I woke up. I only knew that I was extremely glad to be awake.

When I looked at my neighbour her slim back was turned towards me and she was brushing her hair—there was a great deal of it—long, silvery white, silky. She brushed away steadily, rhythmically, for some time. She must have taken great care of it all her life and now there it all was, intact, to comfort and reassure her that she was still herself. Even when she had pinned it up into a loose bun it fell so prettily round her face that it was difficult to think of her as an old lady.

I can't say that we ever became friendly. She told me that she was an Australian, that her name was Peterson, and once she lent me a glossy magazine.

I hadn't been there long when I realized that I didn't like the convalescent home and that the sooner I got out of it the better I'd be pleased. The monotony of the hospital had finally had a soothing effect. I'd felt weak, out of love with life, but resigned and passive; here on the contrary I was anxious, restless and yet it ought to have been a comforting place. The passage outside the ward was carpeted in dark red, dark red curtains hung over the tall window at the far end and the staircase had a spacious look, with its wide shallow steps and broad oak banisters—just the sort of house to get well in, you would have thought. But I felt it shut in, brooding, even threatening in its stolid way.

The matron soon insisted on my taking daily exercise in the garden and another patient usually walked at the same time as I did. She always carried a paper bag of boiled sweets which she'd offer to me as we discussed her operation for gall bladder and my heart attack in detail. But all the time I was thinking that there too the trees drooped in a heavy, melancholy way and the grass was a much darker colour than ordinary grass. Something about the whole place reminded me of a placid citizen, respectable and respected, who would poison anyone disliked or disapproved of at the drop of a hat.

No kind ladies came round with trolleys of books, as they had in the hospital, so one day I asked if it wasn't possible for me to have something to read. I was told that there was a library on the ground floor, "Down the stairs," said the nurse, "and to your left."

When I went in the blinds were drawn and I was in semi-darkness but I was so certain that I wasn't alone that I stopped near the door and felt for the light switch. The room was empty except for a large table in the middle with straightbacked chairs arranged round it, as if for a meal, and a rickety bookcase at the far end. There was no one there. No one? "Oh don't be idiotic," I said aloud and walked past the table. The books leant up against each other disconsolately. They had a forlorn, neglected appearance as though no one had looked at or touched them for years. They would have been less reproachful piled in a heap to be thrown away. Most of them were memoirs or African adventures by early Victorian travellers, in very close print. I didn't look long for I hated turning my back on that table, those chairs and when I saw a torn Tauchnitz paperback by a writer I'd heard of I grabbed it and hurried out as quickly as I could. Nothing would have induced me to go back to that room and I read and re-read the book steadily, never taking in what I was reading, so that now I can't remember the title or what it was about. It was after this that I began counting: "Only eight days more, only six days more."

One morning a trim little man looked into
the ward and asked "Does any lady want a
shampoo or haircut?"

Silence except for a few firm "No thank
yous".

Then Mrs. Peterson said: "Yes, I should
like my hair trimmed, please, if it could be
managed."

"Okay," said the man, "tomorrow morning
at eleven."

When he had gone someone said: "He's
a man's barber, you know."

"I just want it trimmed. I have to be careful about split ends," said the Australian.

Next morning the barber appeared with all
his paraphernalia, put a chair near a basin—
there was no looking glass above it—and
smilingly invited her to sit down. She said
something to him, he nodded and proceeded
while everybody watched covertly. She sat
up and he dried her hair gently. Then he
picked it up in one hand and produced a
large pair of scissors. Snip, snip, and half of
it was lying on the floor. One woman gasped.

Mrs. Peterson put her hand up uneasily
and felt her neck but said nothing. She must
have realized that something was wrong but
couldn't know the extent of the damage of
course, and it all happened very quickly. The
rest went and in a few minutes she had dis-
peared under the dryer while the barber
tidied up. When she paid him he said: "You'll

be glad to be rid of the weight of it, won't you dear?" She didn't answer.

"Cheerio ladies." He went off carrying the hair that he had so carefully collected in a plastic bag.

He hadn't made a very good job of setting what was left and her face looked large, naked and rather plain. She still seemed utterly astonished as she walked back to bed. Then she reached for her handglass and stared at herself for a long time. When I saw how distressed she grew as she looked I whispered: "Don't worry, you'll be surprised how quickly it'll grow again."

"No, there isn't time," she said, turned, pulled the sheet up high and lay so still that I thought she was asleep, but I heard her say, not to me or anybody else, "Nobody will want me now."

During the night I was woken to hear her being violently sick. A nurse hurried to her bed. Next morning it started again, she apologized feebly to the matron who came along to look at her. "I'm so very sorry to trouble you, I'm so very sorry."

All day at intervals it went on, the vomiting, the chokings, the weak child's voice saying: "I'm so sorry, I'm so sorry," and by night they had a screen up round her bed.

I stopped listening to the sounds coming from behind the screen, for one gets used to anything. But when, one morning, I saw that

it had been taken away and that the bed
was empty and tidy I was annoyed to hear
a woman say: "They always take them away
like that. Quietly. In the night."

"These people are so damned gloomy," I
said to myself. "She'll probably get perfectly
well, her hair will grow again and soon look
very pretty."

I'd be leaving the convalescent home the
day after tomorrow. Why wasn't I thinking
of that instead of a story read long ago in
the Blue or Yellow fairy book (perhaps the
Crimson) and the words repeating themselves so unreasonably in my head: "Rapunzel, Rapunzel, let down your hair?"

Who Knows What's Up in the Attic?

She sat in one of a row of deck-chairs with other silent, impassive, elderly people watching the sea. Unlike the sky it was the usual dark grey. But it was calm, the waves making a soothing sound as they rolled in gently.

The beach was empty except for a little boy playing by himself and some way off a man throwing a stick for his dog. Over and over again he threw, over and over again the dog dashed into the water barking, wild with enthusiasm. A cat, now, might get bored even if it could be taught the trick, but dogs must be optimists, thinking every time was the first time. Or perhaps just plain silly.

"I've got the car," and he was in the next deck-chair.

"That's the Atlantic, isn't it?" she asked.

"Of course. What did you think it was?"

"I thought it might be the Bristol Channel."

"No, no. Look." He produced a map. "Here

is the Bristol Channel and here are we. That's
the Atlantic."

"It's very grey," she said.

But driving along a road by the sea she
thought that it was a pleasant little town.
Why shouldn't she take one of those flats
painted yellow or pink, green or blue? Holiday flats, they called themselves. Spend a
week or so here? Then she imagined the town
full of people, cars and coaches. Not the same
thing at all.

Besides—she made so many plans.

When they turned inland he began to sing.
Songs from various operas but not in any
language she knew. Every now and again
he'd stop and explain what it was all about.
"That he sings when he first sees her. This
is when he is dying."

"They always sing when they are dying.
So loud too," she said.

But he went on singing. He had a good
voice. How long was it since she had sat by
a man driving fast and singing? Years and
years. Or was it perhaps only yesterday and
everything that had happened since a strange
dream?

On the day before this one—which was also
yesterday—she'd been sitting in the kitchen
of her cottage looking out of the window at
the dismal sky and listening to the silence.
No farm cart passed. No lorry. When she

heard a soft knock, "That must be Mr. Singh" she thought. Everyone else in the village knocked as if they were trying to batter the ramshackle place down. She kept very still and listened. "Surely he'll think I'm out and go away."

Mr. Singh visited the village at intervals selling blouses, scarves and underclothes; he usually persuaded her to buy something gaudy and useless. It had started one day when she was feeling even more lonely and bored than usual, longing for any distraction; then she saw him fairly often.

"The price is £5 but I will let you have it cheaper. Also I will give you a lucky bead. I am holy man and will pray for you."

"But I don't want it, Mr. Singh."

"Don't say that. Don't say that. You break my heart, you break my heart. You don't have to buy, only look," he'd say gently.

How does he get so much into one suitcase, she'd wonder.

"Goodbye mam, thank you mam, God bless you mam." He always called her mam or mum.

She remembered that the door wasn't bolted. "He'll walk in and look for me," she thought. And decided to go into the passage, shake her head at him through the glass top and turn the key.

But instead of the white turban and black

beard that she expected, a strange young man in grey was waiting patiently outside.

"I'm Jan—" he said smiling. "I wrote. Don't you remember? We met last year in London, you gave me your address and said if ever I was in England again I could call on you. Didn't you get my letter?"

Then she remembered the letter from Holland. It was written in English, three pages of it. She'd pored over the difficult handwriting, the passages of unfamiliar poetry. It said that he would be in London and could he come sometime in the afternoon of Tuesday the — of May? She replied that she'd be pleased to see him and added: "But this is a rainy place in the spring."

Tuesday—but this was Monday.

"Of course, of course," she said, trying to sound welcoming. "Do come in. You're just in time for a drink."

But he refused a drink. The sitting-room was dim at this hour and he sat with his back to whatever light there was, talking smoothly and easily about his hotel in Exeter and about the difficulty of finding her place. He was wearing smooth London clothes. He apologized for his English but he had no accent. Every now and then he'd hesitate for a word, that was all.

"You can spend tomorrow with me? Perhaps we could go to the sea. Would you like that?"

"Yes I would. I haven't seen the sea for a long time."

Next morning he'd arrived wearing country clothes and carrying a large bunch of flowers.

"What lovely carnations"; wondering whether she had anything big enough to put them in.

It was when she was sitting next to him in the car that she noticed he was older than she'd thought yesterday and much more attractive.

"You wrote that it always rained here and look what a beautiful day!"

"Oh, isn't it, isn't it?"

Such a beautiful day. The sky pale blue, the clouds light and white and innocent. It seemed ungrateful to remember icy gales, perpetual drizzle. Now the wind was soft and gentle—almost warm. "Winds that blow from the south." Fruit trees covered with flowers were all over the place. As they passed one, she said: "Cherry, plum, I'm not sure."

"I don't know. I am not a country man. I am a city man."

"Yes I can see that," she said.

She was surprised at the security and happiness she felt. She very seldom felt safe or happy and if it was so for this man whom she'd only met briefly once over a drink and never expected to see again, why pull it to pieces?

All the same his face was so familiar. Then

she remembered that life of Modigliani and
the photograph on the cover. He was almost
exactly like it.

When he asked: "Are you getting tired?"

"Well—I'll be glad to get home and have
a drink."

"Yes. But do you mind if we go by Exeter
so that I can pick up some wine that I think
you will like at my hotel?"

When he came out of the hotel he was
carrying two bottles of rosé. They drove back
home quickly along an empty road, hardly
speaking.

"I'll get the glasses? Ice? Or shall I put the
bottles in the fridge for a bit?"

"They're still quite cool," he said. "Feel."

She sat facing the light while he opened a
bottle, lit two cigarettes and gave her one.
Then he took up a book of Dutch poems on
the table. "You read Dutch?"

"No. The English translation's inside. I
can't read Dutch or speak it."

"But you know Amsterdam?"

"A little. Not well. The Hague better. I
remember the canals of course and some
beautiful old houses. But that was a long
time ago. Are the houses still there, I
wonder?"

"Yes, some are still there. And in one lives
my uncle and his sister."

"Oh, does he?"

"Yes, and every evening they invite friends

and play cards up to all hours. Two, three in the morning you can ring them up and they are still playing."

She liked his face when he spoke about these people. Amused but pleased and affectionate. It was nice of him to think of them like that.

"Do they play for money or for love?" she said.

"For love. For love. You know," he said "I admire my uncle. When I was quite a little boy and my mother died he really brought me up. That was in Indonesia. My father is an artist. I have some pictures of his that I like very much and I like him. But he is too —too soft. That is not a good thing."

"I suppose not."

"My uncle is not so." He took a case from his pocket and handed her a small photograph. "That is my uncle."

The uncle looked a bit on the sly side to her.

"I see what you mean," she said.

"And this is my father."

"You are like him."

"Yes I know. And I am fond of him, I feel affection for him but he is not—how do you say—forcible enough."

"Yes, but if everybody were forcible, what a shambles. Don't you think it's quite bad enough as it is?"

He put the photographs away carefully.

"I am sad that I have to go to London to-morrow."

"So am I," she said.

Then, leaning back, he said suddenly: "Tell me—what do you like best about me?"

She was surprised but answered at once. "I like your eyebrows best."

"My eyebrows," he said. "My eyebrows?"

He seemed so astonished that she explained. "You see in a face like yours one expects, or I expect, smooth eyebrows. Black, almost as if they were painted. But yours are shaggy and in the sun they are a good deal lighter than your hair. It's a surprise and I like it very much."

"No one's ever told me that before."

They looked steadily at each other for a few seconds then together they began to laugh.

"Oh I must have a photograph of you like that. I'll get my camera, it's in the car."

"No, don't photograph me. I hate it. I've never liked it all that much, now of course it's a phobia. Please don't."

"Of course not, if you don't wish it. All the same I'd like to take a few photographs of the cottage if you allow me."

"Photograph anything you like, but not me."

At the door he turned. "We recognized each other, didn't we?"

She didn't answer. She thought: yes, I

recognized you almost at once. But I never imagined that you recognized me.

She sat so often in this chair looking at the eternal drizzle, listening to the wind. All night it whistled and whined and moaned, rattled the doors and windows till she had to get up and wedge them with newspapers before she could sleep. All day it tormented the trees. How she'd grown to hate it, the bullying treacherous wind. Even when it wasn't raining, sunshine was just a pale glare.

But today the sun was real sun and the light gold. The grass was yellow, not green. No wonder she felt as if she were in another time, another place, another country. She saw him walking about the field in front of the sitting-room and thought: "What on earth has he found to photograph there? The cows over the hedge?"

"I'm afraid that field is rough and full of holes. I can't garden much."

"I like it today but perhaps on a wet dark day it might be sad. But of course you have many friends."

"Well not exactly. Not in the village anyway. This is a big county, you know."

"So you are alone here. That should not be."

"No, no, I'm all right. A very nice woman comes quite often and I've got a telephone. Besides, I like being alone. Not always of course, but one can't have everything."

"And in the winter, are you alone in the winter?"

"I try to get away for the worst months and then—well it's all a bit chancy."

"I was thinking, I know a place in Italy that you would like very much. It's quiet and beautiful."

"It sounds just the thing."

"And would you think of going there?"

"Why not?" she said. Of course she could think.

Looking worried he said: "I couldn't be with you all the time. I would be with you as often as I could. But you see there is my job. And there is my wife."

"Of course."

"My wife and I don't get on."

"Oh dear, what a pity."

"Yes, we have agreed to stay together for the children till they are older. Meanwhile we don't interfere with each other."

It seemed to her she'd heard that one before, long ago when everything was different. "It sounds a good arrangement—very fair to everybody—" she said. "And maybe. . . ."

"You don't know my wife."

"No."

"She is like this." Now he was getting excited. "I was in New York a few months ago. I brought her back a dress—very pretty. I thought to please her but it hangs in her cupboard. She has never once put it on."

"Perhaps it doesn't fit," she said.

"Of course it fits her, of course. Such a mistake I would not make. She won't wear it because I bought it and she is like that about everything. She wants to separate as much as I do, believe me, but we have this arrangement because of the children. And so. . . ."

"I was only joking."

"But I am not joking at all. I mean what I say."

"Yes and it would be lovely, but it's quite impossible, I can't."

"Why not?"

Of course he must have seen perfectly well why not and if he didn't she was certainly not going to spell it out. That would have depressed her for days, for weeks. How few people understand what a tightrope she walked or what would happen if she slipped. The abyss. Despair. All those things.

She made the first excuse that came into her head. "Such a fuss. My passport. Besides, I hate packing."

"I will come and fetch you. I can come in October. I can pack very well. Nothing will be difficult, you will see."

"You don't know how much I'd like it but really it's just not possible."

He said nothing for a bit, then: "Well think about it. If you change your mind will you write to me? You have my address."

"I'll probably think about it a lot. But I won't change my mind."

"No one is ever certain of that," he said and talked of other things. But when he asked her to dine with him she was obliged to excuse herself for suddenly she was very tired, hardly able to move, too tired to say much.

"Thank you for seeing me and for today," he said at the door, again bowing and kissing her hand. "I will hope to hear from you. Have nice conversations with the cows in the next field."

"You never know," she said.

Before getting into the car he waved and called, "You will see me again."

"Yes, yes, that would be splendid. Try to manage it."

She went back into the kitchen and shut her eyes. "Why not, why not? Why shouldn't I walk out of this place, so dependent on the weather, so meanly built, for poor people. Just four small rooms and an attic. Like my life." She put her hand to her head and laughed. "And who knows what's up in the attic? Not I for one. I wouldn't dare look."

A small house—it was suffocating. She went to the door and propped it open. Why not? Why not? Hadn't she forgotten her one advantage now? She could do exactly what she liked. She could do something a thousand times sillier than taking a holiday in Italy—that is all it was—no one need know and no one would care. Or rather she could easily arrange that no one knew. And most certainly no one would care.

A voice said: "I hope I do not disturb you. I saw your door was open and I came in. I have got this specially for you."

She wiped her eyes hastily. "You are not disturbing me at all. I was nearly asleep." She was delighted to see Mr. Singh. Any port in a storm. "What have you brought to show me today? But let me see it in here."

"This I thought is for you. Beautiful stuff, beautiful. Feel it."

"Yes. But what's that orange-coloured thing?"

"That is a—" He showed it. A short nylon nightgown. Looks a good shape. No lace.

"Pretty," she said.

Looking rather surprised, he held it deftly under her chin. "A very good colour for you," he said. "And I have a black one the same."

When he told her the price of them both she paid him. He didn't try to sell her anything else but shut the suitcase.

She went with him to the door. The wind was getting up and it had turned cold. It won't be fine tomorrow, she thought.

"Goodbye mam, thank you mam, I will pray for you."

"You do just that," she said. And locked the door.

Sleep It Off, Lady

One October afternoon Mrs. Baker was having tea with Miss Verney and talking about the proposed broiler factory in the middle of the village where they both lived. Miss Verney, who had not been listening attentively, said, "You know Letty, I've been thinking a great deal about death lately. I hardly ever do, strangely enough."

"No dear," said Mrs. Baker. "It isn't strange at all. It's quite natural. We old people are rather like children, we live in the present as a rule. A merciful dispensation of providence."

"Perhaps," said Miss Verney doubtfully.

Mrs. Baker said "we old people" quite kindly, but could not help knowing that while she herself was only sixty-three and might, with any luck, see many a summer (after many a summer dies the swan, as some man said), Miss Verney, certainly well over seventy, could hardly hope for anything of the sort. Mrs. Baker gripped the arms of her chair. "Many a summer, touch wood and please God," she thought. Then she remarked that it was getting dark so early now and wasn't it extraordinary how time flew.

Miss Verney listened to the sound of the car driving away, went back to her sitting-room and looked out of the window at the flat fields, the apple trees, the lilac tree that wouldn't flower again, not for ten years they told her, because lilacs won't stand being pruned. In the distance there was a rise in the ground—you could hardly call it a hill—and three trees so exactly shaped and spaced that they looked artificial. "It would be rather lovely covered in snow," Miss Verney thought. "The snow, so white, so smooth and in the end so boring. Even the hateful shed wouldn't look so bad." But she'd made up her mind to forget the shed.

Miss Verney had decided that it was an eyesore when she came to live in the cottage. Most of the paint had worn off the once-black galvanized iron. Now it was a greenish colour. Part of the roof was loose and flapped noisily in windy weather and a small gate off its hinges leaned up against the entrance. Inside it was astonishingly large, the far end almost dark. "What a waste of space," Miss Verney thought. "That must come down." Strange that she hadn't noticed it before.

Nails festooned with rags protruded from

the only wooden rafter. There was a tin
bucket with a hole, a huge dustbin. Nettles
flourished in one corner but it was the opposite corner which disturbed her. Here was
piled a rusty lawnmower, an old chair with
a carpet draped over it, several sacks, and
the remains of what had once been a bundle
of hay. She found herself imagining that a
fierce and dangerous animal lived there and
called aloud: "Come out, come out, Shredni
Vashtar, the beautiful." Then rather alarmed
at herself she walked away as quickly as she
could.

But she was not unduly worried. The local
builder had done several odd jobs for her
when she moved in and she would speak to
him when she saw him next.

"Want the shed down?" said the builder.

"Yes," said Miss Verney. "It's hideous, and
it takes up so much space."

"It's on the large side," the builder said.

"Enormous. Whatever did they use it for?"

"I expect it was the garden shed."

"I don't care what it was," said Miss Verney. "I want it out of the way."

The builder said that he couldn't manage
the next week, but the Monday after that
he'd look in and see what could be done.
Monday came and Miss Verney waited but
he didn't arrive. When this had happened
twice she realized that he didn't mean to
come and wrote to a firm in the nearest town.

A few days later a cheerful young man knocked at the door, explained who he was and asked if she would let him know exactly what she wanted. Miss Verney, who wasn't feeling at all well, pointed, "I want that pulled down. Can you do it?"

The young man inspected the shed, walked round it, then stood looking at it.

"I want it destroyed," said Miss Verney passionately, "utterly destroyed and carted away. I hate the sight of it."

"Quite a job," he said candidly.

And Miss Verney saw what he meant. Long after she was dead and her cottage had vanished it would survive. The tin bucket and the rusty lawnmower, the pieces of rag fluttering in the wind. All would last for ever.

Eyeing her rather nervously he became businesslike. "I see what you want, and of course we can let you have an estimate of the cost. But you realize that if you pull the shed down you take away from the value of your cottage?"

"Why?" said Miss Verney.

"Well," he said, "very few people would live here without a car. It could be converted into a garage easily or even used as it is. You can decide of course when you have the estimate whether you think it worth the expense and . . . the trouble. Good day."

Left alone, Miss Verney felt so old, lonely and helpless that she began to cry. No builder would tackle that shed, not for any price she could afford. But crying relieved her and she soon felt quite cheerful again. It was ridiculous to brood, she told herself. She quite liked the cottage. One morning she'd wake up and know what to do about the shed, meanwhile she wouldn't look at the thing. She wouldn't think about it.

But it was astonishing how it haunted her dreams. One night she was standing looking at it changing its shape and becoming a very smart, shiny, dark blue coffin picked out in white. It reminded her of a dress she had once worn. A voice behind her said: "That's the laundry."

"Then oughtn't I to put it away?" said Miss Verney in her dream.

"Not just yet. Soon," said the voice so loudly that she woke up.

She had dragged the large dustbin to the entrance and, because it was too heavy for her to lift, had arranged for it to be carried to the gate every week for the dustmen to collect. Every morning she took a small yellow bin from under the sink and emptied it into the large dustbin, quickly, without lingering or looking around. But on one particular morning the usual cold wind had dropped and she stood wondering if a coat of white paint would improve matters. Paint might look a lot worse. Besides who could she get to do it? Then she saw a cat, as she thought, walking slowly across the far end. The sun shone through a chink in the wall. It was a large rat. Horrified, she watched it disappear under the old chair, dropped the yellow bin, walked as fast as she was able up the road and knocked at the door of a shabby thatched cottage.

"Oh Tom. There are rats in my shed. I've just seen a huge one. I'm so desperately afraid of them. What shall I do?"

When she left Tom's cottage she was still shaken, but calmer. Tom had assured her that he had an infallible rat poison, arrangements had been made, his wife had supplied a strong cup of tea.

He came that same day to put down the poison, and when afterwards he rapped loudly on the door and shouted: "Everything under control?" she answered quite cheerfully, "Yes, I'm fine and thanks for coming."

As one sunny day followed another she almost forgot how much the rat had frightened her. "It's dead or gone away," she assured herself.

When she saw it again she stood and stared disbelieving. It crossed the shed in the same unhurried way and she watched, not able to move. A huge rat, there was no doubt about it.

This time Miss Verney didn't rush to Tom's

cottage to be reassured. She managed to get
to the kitchen, still holding the empty yellow
pail, slammed the door and locked it. Then
she shut and bolted all the windows. This
done, she took off her shoes, lay down, pulled
the blankets over her head and listened to
her hammering heart.

> *I'm the monarch of all I survey.*
> *My right, there is none to dispute.*

That was the way the rat walked.

In the close darkness she must have dozed,
for suddenly she was sitting at a desk in the
sun copying proverbs into a ruled book: "Evil
Communications corrupt good manners. Look
before you leap. Patience is a virtue, good
temper a blessing," all the way up to Z. Z
would be something to do with zeal or zeal-
ous. But how did they manage about X? What
about X?

Thinking this, she slept, then woke, put on
the light, took two tuinal tablets and slept
again, heavily. When she next opened her
eyes it was morning, the unwound bedside
clock had stopped, but she guessed the time
from the light and hurried into the kitchen
waiting for Tom's car to pass. The room was
stuffy and airless but she didn't dream of
opening the window. When she saw the car
approaching she ran out into the road and
waved it down. It was as if fear had given

her wings and once more she moved lightly
and quickly.

"Tom. Tom."

He stopped.

"Oh Tom, the rat's still there. I saw it last
evening."

He got down stiffly. Not a young man, but
surely, surely, a kind man? "I put down
enough stuff to kill a dozen rats," he said.
"Let's 'ave a look."

He walked across to the shed. She followed,
several yards behind, and watched him rattling the old lawnmower, kicking the sacks,
trampling the hay and nettles.

"No rat 'ere," he said at last.

"Well there was one," she said.

"Not 'ere."

"It was a huge rat," she said.

Tom had round brown eyes, honest eyes,
she'd thought. But now they were sly, mock-
ing, even hostile.

"Are you sure it wasn't a pink rat?" he said.

She knew that the bottles in her dustbin
were counted and discussed in the village.
But Tom, who she liked so much?

"No," she managed to say steadily. "An
ordinary colour but very large. Don't they
say that some rats now don't care about
poison? Super rats."

Tom laughed. "Nothing of that sort around
'ere."

She said: "I asked Mr. Slade, who cuts the

grass, to clear out the shed and he said he
would but I think he's forgotten."

"Mr. Slade is a very busy man," said Tom.
"He can't clear out the shed just when you
tell him. You've got to wait. Do you expect
him to leave his work and waste his time
looking for what's not there?"

"No," she said, "of course not. But I think it
ought to be done." (She stopped herself from
saying: "I can't because I'm afraid.")

"Now you go and make yourself a nice cup
of tea," Tom said, speaking in a more friendly
voice. "There's no rat in your shed." And he
went back to his car.

Miss Verney slumped heavily into the
kitchen armchair. "He doesn't believe me. I
can't stay alone in this place, not with that
monster a few yards away. I can't do it." But
another cold voice persisted: "Where will you
go? With what money? Are you really such
a coward as all that?"

After a time Miss Verney got up. She dragged
what furniture there was away from the walls
so that she would know that nothing lurked
in the corners and decided to keep the windows looking onto the shed shut and bolted.
The others she opened but only at the top.
Then she made a large parcel of all the food
that the rat could possibly smell—cheese,
bacon, ham, cold meat, practically every-

thing . . . she'd give it to Mrs. Randolph, the cleaning woman, later.

"But no more confidences." Mrs. Randolph would be as sceptical as Tom had been. A nice woman but a gossip, she wouldn't be able to resist telling her cronies about the giant, almost certainly imaginary, rat terrorizing her employer.

Next morning Mrs. Randolph said that a stray dog had upset the large dustbin. She'd had to pick everything up from the floor of the shed. "It wasn't a dog" thought Miss Verney, but she only suggested that two stones on the lid turned the other way up would keep the dog off.

When she saw the size of the stones she nearly said aloud: "I defy any rat to get that lid off."

Miss Verney had always been a careless, not a fussy, woman. Now all that changed. She spent hours every day sweeping, dusting, arranging the cupboards and putting fresh paper into the drawers. She pounced on every speck of dust with a dustpan. She tried to convince herself that as long as she kept her house spotlessly clean the rat would keep to the shed, not to wonder what she would do if, after all, she encountered it.

"I'd collapse," she thought, "that's what I'd do."

After this she'd start with fresh energy,

again fearfully sweeping under the bed, behind cupboards. Then feeling too tired to eat, she would beat up an egg in cold milk, add a good deal of whisky and sip it slowly. "I don't need a lot of food now." But her work in the house grew slower and slower, her daily walks shorter and shorter. Finally the walks stopped. "Why should I bother?" As she never answered letters, letters ceased to arrive, and when Tom knocked at the door one day to ask how she was: "Oh I'm quite all right," she said and smiled.

He seemed ill at ease and didn't speak about rats or clearing the shed out. Nor did she.

"Not seen you about lately," he said.

"Oh I go the other way now."

When she shut the door after him she thought: "And I imagined I liked him. How very strange."

"No pain?" the doctor asked.

"It's just an odd feeling," said Miss Verney.

The doctor said nothing. He waited.

"It's as if all my blood was running backwards. It's rather horrible really. And then for a while sometimes I can't move. I mean if I'm holding a cup I have to drop it because there's no life in my arm."

"And how long does that last?"

"Not long. Only a few minutes I suppose. It just seems a long time."

"Does it happen often?"

"Twice lately."

The doctor thought he'd better examine her. Eventually he left the room and came back with a bottle half full of pills. "Take these three times a day—don't forget, it's important. Long before they're finished I'll come and see you. I'm going to give you some injections that may help, but I'll have to send away for those."

As Miss Verney was gathering her things together before leaving the surgery he asked in a casual voice: "Are you on the telephone?"

"No," said Miss Verney, "but I have an arrangement with some people."

"You told me. But those people are some way off, aren't they?"

"I'll get a telephone," said Miss Verney making up her mind. "I'll see about it at once."

"Good. You won't be so lonely."

"I suppose not."

"Don't go moving the furniture about, will you? Don't lift heavy weights. Don't . . ." ("Oh Lord," she thought, "is he going to say 'Don't drink!'—because that's impossible!") . . . "Don't worry," he said.

When Miss Verney left his surgery she felt relieved but tired and she walked very slowly home. It was quite a long walk for she lived in the less prosperous part of the village, near the row of council houses. She had never minded that. She was protected by tall thick hedges and a tree or two. Of course it had taken her some time to get used to the children's loud shrieking and the women who stood outside their doors to gossip. At first they stared at her with curiosity and some disapproval, she couldn't help feeling, but they'd soon found out that she was harmless.

The child Deena, however, was a very different matter.

Most of the village boys were called Jack, Willie, Stan and so on—the girls' first names were more elaborate. Deena's mother had gone one better than anyone else and christened her daughter Undine.

Deena—as everyone called her—was a tall plump girl of about twelve with a pretty, healthy but rather bovine face. She never joined the shrieking games, she never played football with dustbin lids. She apparently spent all her spare time standing at the gate of her mother's house silently, unsmilingly, staring at everyone who passed.

Miss Verney had long ago given up trying to be friendly. So much did the child's cynical eyes depress her that she would cross over the road to avoid her, and sometimes was guilty of the cowardice of making sure Deena wasn't there before setting out.

Now she looked anxiously along the street and was relieved that it was empty. "Of

course," she told herself, "it's getting cold.
When winter comes they'll all stay indoors."

Not that Deena seemed to mind cold. Only
a few days ago, looking out of the window,
Miss Verney had seen her standing outside—
oblivious of the bitter wind—staring at the
front door as though, if she looked hard
enough, she could see through the wood and
find out what went on in the silent house—
what Miss Verney did with herself all day.

One morning soon after her visit to the doctor Miss Verney woke feeling very well and
very happy. Also she was not at all certain
where she was. She lay luxuriating in the
feeling of renewed youth, renewed health,
and slowly recognized the various pieces of
furniture.

"Of course," she thought when she drew
the curtains. "What a funny place to end up
in."

The sky was pale blue. There was no wind.
Watching the still trees she sang softly to
herself: "The day of days." She had always
sung "The day of days" on her birthday.
Poised between two years—last year, next
year—she never felt any age at all. Birthdays
were a pause, a rest.

In the midst of slow dressing she remembered the rat for the first time. But that
seemed something that had happened long
ago. "Thank God I didn't tell anybody else

how frightened I was. As soon as they give
me a telephone I'll ask Letty Baker to tea.
She'll know exactly the sensible thing to do."

Out of habit she ate, swept and dusted
but even more slowly than usual and with
long pauses, when leaning on the handle of
her tall, old-fashioned, carpet sweeper she
stared out at the trees. "Goodbye summer.
Goodbye goodbye," she hummed. But in spite
of sad songs she never lost the certainty of
health, of youth.

All at once she noticed, to her surprise,
that it was getting dark. "And I haven't
emptied the dustbin."

She got to the shed carrying the small yellow plastic pail and saw that the big dustbin
wasn't there. For once Mrs. Randolph must
have slipped up and left it outside the gate.
Indeed it was so.

She first brought in the lid, easy, then
turned the heavy bin onto its side and kicked
it along. But this was slow. Growing im-
patient, she picked it up, carried it into the
shed and looked for the stones that had de-
feated the dog, the rat. They too were miss-
ing and she realized that Mrs. Randolph, a
hefty young woman in a hurry, must have
taken out the bin, stones and all. They would
be in the road where the dustmen had thrown
them. She went to look and there they were.

She picked up the first stone, and astonished at its weight, immediately dropped it.

But lifted it again and staggered to the shed, then leaned breathless against the cold wall. After a few minutes she breathed more easily, was less exhausted and the determination to prove to herself that she was quite well again drove her into the road to pick up the second stone.

After a few steps she felt that she had been walking for a long time, for years, weighed down by an impossible weight, and now her strength was gone and she couldn't any more. Still, she reached the shed, dropped the stone and said: "That's all now, that's the lot. Only the yellow plastic pail to tackle." She'd fix the stones tomorrow. The yellow pail was light, full of paper, eggshells, stale bread. Miss Verney lifted it. . . .

She was sitting on the ground with her back against the dustbin and her legs stretched out, surrounded by torn paper and eggshells. Her skirt had ridden up and there was a slice of stale bread on her bare knee. She felt very cold and it was nearly dark.

"What happened," she thought, "did I faint or something? I must go back to the house."

She tried to get up but it was as if she were glued to the ground. "Wait," she thought. "Don't panic. Breathe deeply. Relax." But when she tried again she was lead. "This has happened before. I'll be all right soon," she told herself. But darkness was coming on very quickly.

Some women passed on the road and she called to them. At first: "Could you please . . . I'm so sorry to trouble you . . ." but the wind had got up and was blowing against her and no one heard. "Help!" she called. Still no one heard.

Tightly buttoned up, carrying string bags, heads in headscarves, they passed and the road was empty.

With her back against the dustbin, shivering with cold, she prayed: "God, don't leave me here. Dear God, let someone come. Let someone come!"

When she opened her eyes she was not at all surprised to see a figure leaning on her gate.

"Deena! Denna!" she called, trying to keep the hysterical relief out of her voice.

Deena advanced cautiously, stood a few yards off and contemplated Miss Verney lying near the dustbin with an expressionless face.

"Listen Deena," said Miss Verney. "I'm afraid I'm not very well. Will you please ask your mother—your mum—to telephone to the doctor. He'll come I think. And if only she could help me back into the house. I'm very cold. . . ."

Deena said: "It's no good my asking mum. She doesn't like you and she doesn't want to have anything to do with you. She hates stuck

up people. Everybody knows that you shut
yourself up to get drunk. People can hear you
falling about. 'She ought to take more water
with it,' my mum says. Sleep it off, lady,"
said this horrible child, skipping away.

Miss Verney didn't try to call her back or
argue. She knew that it was useless. A numb
weak feeling slowly took possession of her.
Stronger than cold. Stronger than fear. It was
a great unwillingness to do anything more at
all—it was almost resignation. Even if someone else came, would she call again for help.
Could she? Fighting the cold numbness she
made a last tremendous effort to move, at any
rate to jerk the bread off her knee, for now
her fear of the rat, forgotten all day, began
to torment her.

It was impossible.

She strained her eyes to see into the corner
where it would certainly appear—the corner
with the old chair and carpet, the corner with
the bundle of hay. Would it attack at
once or would it wait until it was sure that
she couldn't move? Sooner or later it would
come. So Miss Verney waited in the darkness
for the Super Rat.

It was the postman who found her. He had
a parcel of books for her and he left them as
usual in the passage. But he couldn't help
noticing that all the lights were on and all

the doors open. Miss Verney was certainly not in the cottage.

"I suppose she's gone out. But so early and such a cold morning?"

Uneasy, he looked back at the gate and saw the bundle of clothes near the shed.

He managed to lift her and got her into the kitchen armchair. There was an open bottle of whisky on the table and he tried to force her to drink some, but her teeth were tightly clenched and the whisky spilled all over her face.

He remembered that there was a telephone in the house where he was to deliver next. He must hurry.

In less time than you'd think, considering it was a remote village, the doctor appeared and shortly afterwards the ambulance.

Miss Verney died that evening in the nearest hospital without recovering consciousness. The doctor said she died of shock and cold. He was treating her for a heart condition, he said.

"Very widespread now—a heart condition."

I Used to
Live Here Once

She was standing by the river looking at
the stepping stones and remembering each
one. There was the round unsteady stone, the
pointed one, the flat one in the middle—the
safe stone where you could stand and look
around. The next wasn't so safe for when the
river was full the water flowed over it and
even when it showed dry it was slippery. But
after that it was easy and soon she was standing on the other side.

The road was much wider than it used to
be but the work had been done carelessly.
The felled trees had not been cleared away
and the bushes looked trampled. Yet it was
the same road and she walked along feeling
extraordinarily happy.

It was a fine day, a blue day. The only
thing was that the sky had a glassy look that
she didn't remember. That was the only word
she could think of. Glassy. She turned the
corner, saw that what had been the old pavé

had been taken up, and there too the road
was much wider, but it had the same un-
finished look.

She came to the worn stone steps that led
up to the house and her heart began to beat.
The screw pine was gone, so was the mock
summer house called the ajoupa, but the
clove tree was still there and at the top of the
steps the rough lawn stretched away, just as
she remembered it. She stopped and looked
towards the house that had been added to
and painted white. It was strange to see a
car standing in front of it.

There were two children under the big
mango tree, a boy and a little girl, and she
waved to them and called "Hello" but they
didn't answer her or turn their heads. Very
fair children, as Europeans born in the West
Indies so often are: as if the white blood is
asserting itself against all odds.

The grass was yellow in the hot sunlight
as she walked towards them. When she was
quite close she called again, shyly: "Hello."
Then, "I used to live here once," she said.

Still they didn't answer. When she said
for the third time "Hello" she was quite near
them. Her arms went out instinctively with
the longing to touch them.

It was the boy who turned. His grey eyes
looked straight into hers. His expression
didn't change. He said: "Hasn't it gone cold

all of a sudden. D'you notice? Let's go in."

"Yes let's," said the girl.

Her arms fell to her sides as she watched them running across the grass to the house. That was the first time she knew.

ALL TIME BESTSELLERS
FROM POPULAR LIBRARY

☐ THE BERLIN CONNECTION—Simmel	08607-6	1.95
☐ THE BEST PEOPLE—Van Slyke	08456-1	1.75
☐ A BRIDGE TOO FAR—Ryan	08373-5	2.50
☐ THE CAESAR CODE—Simmel	08413-8	1.95
☐ DO BLACK PATENT LEATHER SHOES REALLY REFLECT UP?—Powers	08490-1	1.75
☐ ELIZABETH—Hamilton	04013-0	1.75
☐ THE FURY—Farris	08620-3	2.25
☐ THE HAB THEORY—Eckerty	08597-5	2.50
☐ HARDACRE—Skelton	04026-2	2.25
☐ THE HEART LISTENS—Van Slyke	08520-7	1.95
☐ TO KILL A MOCKINGBIRD—Lee	08376-X	1.50
☐ THE LAST BATTLE—Ryan	08381-6	2.25
☐ THE LAST CATHOLIC IN AMERICA—Powers	08528-2	1.50
☐ THE LONGEST DAY—Ryan	08380-8	1.95
☐ LOVE'S WILD DESIRE—Blake	08616-5	1.95
☐ THE MIXED BLESSING—Van Slyke	08491-X	1.95
☐ MORWENNA—Goring	08604-1	1.95
☐ THE RICH AND THE RIGHTEOUS —Van Slyke	08585-1	1.95

Buy them at your local bookstores or use this handy coupon for ordering: